TACTICAL MAGIK
(IMMORTAL OPS)

MANDY M. ROTH

Published by Raven Books
www.ravenhappyhour.com

SUGGESTED READING ORDER OF BOOKS RELEASED TO DATE IN THE IMMORTAL OPS SERIES WORLD

This list is NOT up to date. Please check MandyRoth.com for the most current release list.

Suggested reading order of books released to

date in the

Immortal Ops Series world

Immortal Ops

Critical Intelligence

Radar Deception

Strategic Vulnerability

Tactical Magik

Act of Mercy

Administrative Control

Act of Surrender

Broken Communication

Separation Zone

Act of Submission

Damage Report

Act of Command

Wolf's Surrender

The Dragon Shifter's Duty

Midnight Echoes

Isolated Maneuver

Expecting Darkness

Area of Influence

More to come (check www.mandyroth.com for new releases)

Books in each series within the Immortal Ops World.

This list is NOT up to date. To see an updated list of the books within each series under the umbrella of the Immortal Ops World please visit MandyRoth.com. Mandy is always releasing new books within the series world. Sign up for her newsletter at MandyRoth.com to never miss a new release.

You can read each individual series within the world, in whatever order you want…

PSI-Ops:

Act of Mercy
Act of Surrender
Act of Submission
Act of Command
Act of Passion
And more (see Mandy's website & sign up for
her newsletter for notification of releases)

Immortal Ops:

Immortal Ops
Critical Intelligence
Radar Deception
Strategic Vulnerability
Tactical Magik
Administrative Control
Separation Zone
Area of Influence
And more...
(see Mandy's website & sign up for her
newsletter for notification of releases)

Immortal Outcasts:

Broken Communication
Damage Report
Isolated Maneuver
And more…
(see Mandy's website & sign up for her
newsletter for notification of releases)

Shadow Agents:

Wolf's Surrender
The Dragon Shifter's Duty
And more…
(see Mandy's website & sign up for her
newsletter for notification of releases)

Crimson Ops Series:

Midnight Echoes
Expecting Darkness
And more…

(see Mandy's website & sign up for her newsletter for notification of releases)

Paranormal Regulators Series and Clear Sight Division Operatives (Part of the Immortal Ops World) Coming Soon!

with the smoldering heat that readers can expect from Ms. Roth. Put it on your hot list…and keep it there! —The Road to Romance

5 Stars—*Her characters are so realistic, I find myself wondering about the fine line between fact and fiction… This was one captivating tale that I did not want to end. Just the right touch of humor endeared these characters to me even more*—eCataRomance Reviews

5 Steamy Cups of Coffee—*Combining the world of secret government operations with mythical creatures as if they were an everyday thing, she (Ms. Roth) then has the audacity to make you actually believe it and wonder if there could be some truth to it. I know I did. Nora Roberts once told me that there are some people who are good writers and some who are good storytellers, but the best is a combination of both and I believe Ms. Roth is just that. Mandy Roth never fails to surpass herself* —coffeetimeromance

Mandy Roth kicks ass in this story —inthelibraryreview

Immortal Ops (I-Ops) Team Members

Lukian Vlakhusha: Alpha-Dog-One. Team captain, werewolf, King of the Lycans. Book: Immortal Ops (Immortal Ops)

Geoffroi (Roi) Majors: Alpha-Dog-Two. Second-in-command, werewolf, blood-bound brother to Lukian. Book: Critical Intelligence (Immortal Ops)

Doctor Thaddeus Green: Bravo-Dog-One. Scientist, tech guru, werepanther. Book: Radar Deception (Immortal Ops)

Jonathon (Jon) Reynell: Bravo-Dog-Two. Sniper, weretiger. Book: Separation Zone (Immortal Ops)

Wilson Rousseau: Bravo-Dog-Three. Resident smart-ass, wererat. Book: Strategic Vulnerability (Immortal Ops)

Eadan Daly: Alpha-Dog-Three. PSI-Op and handler on loan to the I-Ops to round out the team, Fae. Book: Tactical Magik (Immortal Ops)

Lance Toov: Werepanther and vampire hybrid. Book: Area of Influence (Immortal Ops)

Colonel Asher Brooks: Chief of Operations and point person for the Immortal Ops Team. Book: Administrative Control (Immortal Ops)

Paranormal Security and Intelligence (PSI) Operatives

General Jack C. Newman: Director of Operations for PSI North American Division, werelion. Adoptive father of Missy Carter-Majors

Duke Marlow: PSI-Operative, werewolf. Book: Act of Mercy (PSI-Ops)

Doctor James (Jimmy) Hagen: PSI-Operative, werewolf. Took a ten-year hiatus from PSI. Book: Act of Surrender (PSI-Ops)

Striker (Dougal) McCracken: PSI-Operative, werewolf

Miles (Boomer) Walsh: PSI-Operative,

werepanther. Book: Act of Submission (PSI-Ops)

Captain Corbin Jones: Operations coordinator and captain for PSI-Ops Team Five, werelion. Book: Act of Command (PSI-Ops)

Malik (Tut) Nasser: PSI-Operative, (PSI-Ops)

Colonel Ulric Lovett: Director of Operations, PSI-London Division

Dr. Sambora: PSI-Operative, (PSI-Ops)

Immortal Outcasts

Casey Black: I-Ops test subject, werewolf. Book: Broken Communication

Weston Carol: I-Ops test subject, werebear. Book: Damage Report

Bane Antonov: I-Ops test subject, weregorilla. Book: Isolated Maneuver

Shadow Agents

Bradley Durant: PSI-Ops: Shadow Agent Division, werewolf. Book: Wolf's Surrender

Ezra: PSI-Ops: Shadow Agent Division, dragon-shifter

Caesar: PSI-Ops: Shadow Agent Division, werewolf

Crimson Sentinel Ops Division

Bhaltair: Crimson-Ops: Fang Gang, vampire. Book: Midnight Echoes

Labrainn: Crimson-Ops: Fang Gang, vampire

Auberi Bouchard: Crimson-Ops: Fang Gang, vampire

Searc Macleod: Crimson-Ops: Fang Gang, vampire. Book: Expecting Darkness

Daniel Townsend: Crimson-Ops: Fang Gang, vampire

Blaise Regnier: Crimson-Ops: Fang Gang, vampire

Paranormal Regulators

Stamatis Emathia: Paranormal Regulator, vampire

Whitney: Paranormal Regulator, werewolf

Cormag Buchanan: Paranormal Regulator, master vampire

Erik: Paranormal Regulator, shifter

Shane: Paranormal Regulator, shifter

Miscellaneous

Culann of the Council: Father to Kimberly; Badass Fae

Pierre Molyneux: Master vampire bent on creating a race of super soldiers

Gisbert Krauss: Mad scientist who wants to create a master race of supernaturals

Walter Helmuth: Head of Seattle's paranormal underground. In league with Molyneux and Krauss

Dr. Lakeland Matthews: Scientist, vital role in the creation of a successful Immortal Ops Team. Father to Peren Matthews

Dr. Bertrand: Mad scientist with Donavon Dynamics Corporation (The Corporation)

Tactical Magik (Immortal Ops)
Book Five in the Immortal Ops Series.

Eadan Daly has thrown himself into the role of the sixth Immortal Ops team member, even though it wasn't supposed to be a permanent position, and has forged a brotherhood of sorts with the other men. When he's asked to go on a solo mission for the Paranormal Security and Intelligence Branch—PSI, for short—he's not so sure he wants his old job back.

Inara Nash is a survivor, doing what she must to get by. On the run for years from an organization she doesn't fully understand, she tries to stay under the radar. When a blond hunk arrives and claims he's her savior, she suspects her luck might have finally run out. Sure, he's hot and looks like he'd be good in bed, but there is something almost magikal about him that defies reality. And if there is one thing she's learned during her life in the paranormal underground, it's that you never trust a magik.

DEDICATION

This is a long one. I'm sorry, but this book was a long time coming. I'll start with my author buddies. To Michelle M. Pillow, Jaycee Clark, Melissa Schroeder and Jax Cassidy, thank you for agreeing to be part of the Magical Temptations project. And thanks for understanding when TM had to reach into another series instead. Michelle and Jaycee, you both went above and beyond, listening to me talk about various storylines, yelling at me when I deleted 20k words in thirty seconds, and making me swear to knock that crap off. Thank you!

To Laurann Dohner, thank you for encouraging me to keep reaching for my dream. You're one tough cookie!

To my partner in mischief, Yasmine Galenorn, thank you for talking me off the proverbial ledge and for making me remember to take time for me.

To my proofer, Leah, my editor, Suz, and my final

line editor, Dianne, thank you for fixing "me." And to Suz for taking on this project even with all you have going on.

To the fans of my Immortal Ops Series. Thank you for your continued support for the series over the past ten plus years. I'm honestly having a hard time wrapping my mind around the fact that 2014 will mark the ten-year anniversary of the release of Immortal Ops Book One. I think the saying is true: time does fly when you're having fun.

I know you've been waiting for more installments and I promise you Tactical Magik is the first of many more within the Immortal Ops World. A side note: Tactical Magik picks up one month after Strategic Vulnerability ends. Also, be on the lookout for related spinoff series from the Immortal Ops. I'm sure you can guess PSI-Ops (Paranormal Security and Intelligence Ops) will be headed your way as well as the other Ops team stories. The first is Act of Mercy. Plus, I have many more surprises in store for you all because you're the greatest group of readers an author could ask for. And for my "super fans", I hope you enjoy the crossover into the underground fight club world from my book Going the Distance (Paranormal Death Match).

As for Tactical Magik, I hope you love Eadan's story as much as I do. I know he's different from the other ops, *as he's not a shifter, but he's still kick-ass. And from the bottom of my heart I hope you like how his story demanded it be told. Sometimes, I really do feel I'm at the mercy of the character. His story was a long time coming for me. You all know the Ops hold a special place in my heart.*

Thank you,

Mandy M. Roth

ONE

"I SAID I WAS SORRY," Geoffroi "Roi" Majors stated as he glanced back at Eadan from the front passenger seat of the Hum-V. The vehicle that currently held five not-so-small guys was hardly inconspicuous. It was also less than comfortable. They stuck out like sore thumbs and Eadan Daly had to question the wisdom of this being their getaway vehicle. This one wasn't reinforced to help stop bullets. It seemed a lot like tissue paper at the moment. Pretty much all it had going for it was cool factor. One that screamed government or paramilitary group. A blinking sign on the top would only make it worse.

Shoot here. There is a better than average chance you'll hit your target.

With the entrance Lukian had been forced to make to get to them, they might as well have sent out engraved invitations to the enemy to come shoot at them there. Would have proven as effective.

"This thing go any faster?" Wilson asked, fidgeting in his seat.

Lukian didn't comment. He merely glanced at the rearview mirror. His glare was enough of a response.

Eadan's ears were still ringing from the hail of gunfire around them. Had he not assisted with his magik, they'd be picking lead out of his ass.

Out of all their asses.

He'd expended more power than he should have, but it was required. Unfortunately, he'd be feeling the ill effects of that much usage for probably a week or more. Unless he met up with a hottie at a bar and spent the night rockin' her world. Sexual energy would speed his ability to rebuild his natural-born power base.

He looked to his left at his fellow Immortal Ops (I-Ops) teammates, Jon and Wilson. Jon shook his head, indicating they should not accept *this* apology from Roi either. They'd been steadily rejecting Roi's attempts to make amends for the past twenty minutes.

Wilson tapped his fingers on the doorframe, an annoyed breath easing from his lips. "You left without us. In a hostile zone, mind you. Might as well have painted a damn target on us yourself."

"No," Roi protested, twisting in the seat. His dark hair fell partially onto his face. "I told you already I thought Lukian was getting you. And, see, he got you."

Lukian, the team captain, snorted as he drove. He tended to be on the quiet side yet always managed to get his point across. Eadan had been unsure how to read him at first but was learning more and more each day.

"What?" Roi grunted and tossed his hands in the air. "Fine. I wasn't listening during the briefing because I was exhausted."

Green's voice came over their comms unit earpieces. "Stop worrying. Your wife and your girls will be fine."

Roi shifted around in his seat as he tapped his wrist and spoke into his comms piece. "You're the one who told me it's uncommon for a woman pregnant with twins to go to term.

4 MANDY M. ROTH

That means I could become a father any day now. I'm not ready yet. I only just got the nursery finished. I haven't set up college funds for them yet. I didn't…"

Roi was going to spiral out of control again. He'd been doing that more and more of late. Seemed as if the prospect of fatherhood was going to do what the enemy couldn't —kill him.

Lukian reached over as he continued to drive and touched Roi's arm. "Relax, brother. There is plenty of time for all that."

"Why am I the only one freaking out? Your wife is due soon too," Roi said, sounding frantic.

Eadan held back a groan. All this talk of pregnancies was getting on his last damn nerve.

Green's chuckle echoed through their earpieces. He was currently tucked away in a tiny location the team had preselected as base during their current mission. Green was their eyes and ears on everything else going on, a technical guru who also happened to be the best at patching them up when need be.

"Peren has another two months. Missy, with the twins, probably won't go that long. Melanie has two and half months left and Kim has—"

Wilson leaned forward. "Just under five months left."

Eadan nudged Jon. "Is it just me or have our missions deteriorated into recipe swaps and what-to-expect-when-your-mate-is-expecting moments?"

"No," Jon said, his eyes widening. He looked almost scared, as if he too might catch the bug to discuss upcoming babies. "It's not just you."

"I'm fairly sure we were once feared," Eadan added with a laugh. "Now we're the labor patrol. We make the enemy shake in their boots—well, right after we're done talking about the first signs of contractions."

Wilson shook his head. "No. Not feared. Misunderstood. We were totally misunderstood. And just wait, you two will see what this is like when you meet your mates. Then we'll all laugh at you."

"No," Eadan said. "You'll give us burping tricks to help the kid with gas."

Lukian laughed, obviously enjoying the friendly banter. "You're probably right."

"Oh, I know I am."

Jon groaned as he smiled. It was actually a good sign. Jon hadn't been dealing well with the loss of Lance, an Immortal Ops team member. He'd died seven months prior, and in that time Wilson had been captured and thought dead. Jon blamed himself for not finding Wilson sooner and for not preventing Lance's death. For months the men had been walking on eggshells around Wilson because of the horrible ordeal he'd gone through. He'd been captured and tortured while the rest of the team believed he was dead. Had the women behind the men who called themselves Ops not been so persistent, there was a better than average chance Wilson wouldn't be alive right now. The women had gone after him, forcing the men to follow. They'd all managed to bring him home, alive and well. Wilson even managed to get a wife and son out of the deal.

Jon withdrew a pack of cigarettes from his vest pocket and then materialized a lighter. Eadan never said a word as he put the cigarette in his mouth and went to light it.

Wilson knocked it out of Jon's mouth. "What the hell? When did you start smoking again?"

Jon's amber gaze hardened as he reached for the cigarette.

"*Dad*," Wilson said in a whiny voice, tapping the back of Lukian's chair. "He's smoking."

Lukian looked as if he were trying to find his inner happy place.

"That shit will kill ya," Roi said.

"While the effects of smoking have been proven to be detrimental to humans' health, they have no ill effects on us," Green chimed in.

"Tell them the head and heart story again," Roi said with a wag of his brows.

Wilson shook his head. "I don't give a shit. That crap stinks. You're not doing it in here. I'll smell it on myself all damn day."

Jon's mouth changed shape quickly, his teeth lengthening, the start of a tiger's teeth showing. He gave a soft roar at Wilson.

Wilson smiled wide. "*Dad*, he's trying to eat me."

"Dumbass," Roi said.

"Jon," Lukian interjected. "No eating Wilson. He comes in handy from time to time."

Jon's mouth returned to normal and he propped the cigarette between his lips but didn't light it. He merely looked out the window again, ignoring them all.

Eadan snorted, keeping the mood light, and

tapped the back of Roi's seat. "Try not to forget us next time, all right?"

"I think he wanted to leave *you* on purpose," Wilson offered, a cock-sure grin on his face. "He's still sore you used to bang his wife."

True enough. Eadan and Missy had been married at one point in time. Now they were simply close friends. No stretch of the imagination, since their parents were close and had been since they'd been born. They'd been a constant in one another's life since before Eadan could remember. Though his feelings for her were no longer sexual in nature. They were simply of love—the type of love one has for family.

Roi growled. "Missy would have my damn balls on a platter if I let one hair on *blondie's* head be hurt. She's a mess of hormones and damn scary on a good day. So, uh, let's not tell her I forgot to pick him up. And mention him banging her again and I'll cut your dick off, mouse."

"Hey, you forgot *me* too," Wilson protested. "And I'm a wererat. Get it right, douche."

Roi gave Eadan a hard look and Eadan winked at him. "Used to take baths with your wife when we were little too. Stew on that, asshole."

Wilson lost it. "Ohmygod, brilliant!"

Lukian grumbled. "Great. It will take me weeks to calm him down now, Daly."

"He deserved it," Wilson chimed in. "He left us in hostile territory. Hey." Wilson looked to Eadan. "Are you leaking on me?"

Jon twisted and stared at them. "Do I even want to know?"

"No clue what he's talking about," Eadan added.

Wilson shivered. "Magik. Are you leaking it?"

"No. What you're feeling is residual magik. Can't help it. I had to use a lot to protect us from the bullets whizzing by us." He looked up at the back of Roi's head.

Roi shifted in his seat somewhat and Eadan knew the guy was refusing to turn to look back at him. Eadan felt like he was in high school again with the way the men carried on. He'd gotten used to being called blondie. He couldn't blame them. He did have long, blond hair. And as Roi liked to point out, it was very *pretty*. He snorted. "The maturity in this SUV is awe-inspiring."

"Hey, I'm nearly as old as time," Lukian said from the front.

"Old timer," Eadan shot back, making Lukian laugh. "How many centuries have you been alive?"

"We'll get him a walker for his next birthday," Roi said with a grin. He more than likely would, just to get Lukian going. "He can use when he stands before the masses to talk to his minions."

By minions, Roi meant the rest of the lycans. Lukian was the natural-born king of them. Never acted like royalty though. And Eadan knew royalty because of his family and their connections within the Fae community.

Jon mumbled something and returned to looking out the window, seeming very uninterested in the current conversation. Eadan couldn't blame him. The talk would no doubt spin back around to kids and babies. It seemed to do that all the time anymore. Sure, it was nice most of the team was mated and with families, but none of that changed the fact they still did a dangerous job and their full attention was required for it.

Wilson glanced at Eadan. "Colonel Brooks said you're being pulled for a PSI mission after this. That true?"

Eadan nodded, unsure how he felt about returning to his actual job with Paranormal Security and Intelligence even if just for a short period of time, even if PSI was in desperate need of his services. He'd been with the Immortal Ops longer than anyone had thought he would be. There had been an unspoken "never the two shall meet" rule before Eadan coming aboard. He didn't understand why everything had to be so secretive, but that was the government for you, creating super soldiers when they could, bringing in existing supernaturals and using them all to do their dirty work—missions that didn't exist done by men who didn't exist.

Bet they're shitting themselves now that we're technically intermingling.

Funny how he'd been so upset about being "saddled" with them when he was first assigned to the unit nearly seven months back, but they'd become a family of sorts to him—they were his brothers now. He couldn't imagine going back to solo operative work. Sure, he had close friends within PSI, but Eadan wasn't ever paired with them. And PSI was in the process of doing some major housecleaning since it had become evident not long ago that they had traitors in their midst.

"They get their shit sorted out?" asked Roi, ever the user of great prose.

Jon glanced in Eadan's direction. "Any more rogues turn up?"

"Not that I'm aware of, but I haven't been in the loop in a few months now," he admitted. It wasn't that long ago they had all been forced to watch as Missy took on a group of rogue agents. She'd weeded them out and then kicked the ever-loving shit out of them.

Missy-Bean would do no less.

He snorted. She was tenacious.

Wilson tipped his head. "Sounded like the trouble ran deep over there."

"Yeah."

"Brooks also mentioned it could be a long assignment," Lukian said, worry in his gaze, reflected in the rearview mirror. "You need me to talk with him? I think we should be there to back you on this."

"No," replied Eadan. He appreciated the offer. "It's my job. I'm a PSI agent and a handler. Solo work sort of comes with the territory."

"You're one of us now, brother," Jon corrected, coming out of his daze. His amber eyes held concern. "And if I was you, I wouldn't want any one of those assholes over there to have my back. I wouldn't trust them."

Roi mumbled something derogatory under his breath. Lukian cleared his throat and Roi pressed a smile to his face and glanced in the rearview mirror. "Yeah, one of us."

Eadan stared at Jon. "I'll be fine. And there are some I trust with my life. They're not all bad. Just a few rotten apples got into the bunch."

Jon didn't appear to believe him. Eadan already knew the guy was afraid of losing another team member. And Eadan knew how dangerous his job within PSI was. It had already nearly cost him his life once.

"The women will miss you," Green said over the comms unit. Eadan understood he was voicing the men's feelings as well in a way that deflected from them.

Roi grumbled more. "Yeah, cryin' fucking buckets here."

The other men laughed.

Wilson bumped the back of Roi's seat. "What? Afraid your woman will miss him too much?"

"I know mine will," Green said, reminding them of the fact his wife was Eadan's sister. "If you'd return her calls, you'd hear all about the dream she keeps having. It involves you finding your mate."

"I'll be fine," Eadan managed. He didn't want to talk to Melanie about his possible mate. His sister meant well, but Eadan had no desire to get into the discussion with her—again. "I swear. I'll check in when I'm able. Ops-honor."

Lukian touched his comms unit. "Green, what is our ETA to base?"

"Six minutes, Captain."

Eadan soaked in the knowledge that in six minutes he'd technically be done with this mission and then back to what he knew best. Or what he used to know best, anyways.

———

JON REYNELL GLARED out the window, his unlit cigarette perched on the edge of his lips, wanting to voice more outrage over Eadan being yanked from their team but holding his tongue. Fucking higher-ups always thought they knew best. The higher-ups didn't know shit. Their cluelessness had cost Lance his life and almost cost Wilson his as well. How many of their team members did they need to bury before they understood that, while hard to kill, the I-Ops weren't impervious to death?

As Green had pointed out more than once in the past, a head or heart shot would indeed take them down in a way they wouldn't get back up from. Still, the men who pulled the strings kept doing stupid shit.

Like breaking up the band, even if just temporarily.

They were a well-oiled unit. You didn't mess with that. You didn't touch it. You let it be.

But not *them*. Whoever *they* were.

In all the years Jon had been part of the I-Ops, he'd only known a handful of point people —those who handed them their missions, had them report back and pretended to have some semblance of control over them, all the while keeping the people in power a secret. Colonel Brooks was the most recent. Seemed nice enough, but he was kept in the dark on things too. Jon suspected the man was more than met the eye—more than human.

Just like the I-Ops.

There was something about him that Jon couldn't put his finger on. If he was shifter then he'd learned to mask his scent like the I-Ops had decades ago, and if he was a magik he kept that shielded somehow too. All Jon knew was the man had been the same age, appearance-wise, for the past three decades. That wasn't something that happened in nature.

Colonel Brooks had been surprised by the news of a second Immortal Ops Team. And from what Jon could gather, the colonel had been startled by the number of hybrid super soldiers who had attempted an attack upon the I-Ops facility.

Jon shuddered to think what Roi must have gone through when his mate had been the target of their attacks. Finding out they were fighting hybrids who were part-vampire, part-were, part-whatever-the-fuck someone decided to put in the test tubes had set them all on edge.

The hybrids had failed.

Of course.

When they'd all learned of the second I-Ops team, they began to speculate there might be more teams. Jon couldn't imagine more men being subjected to what they'd all gone through, and how many good men had been lost along the way? They'd been trying to locate them, but so far hadn't had too much free time with as busy as Gisbert Krauss and his army of mutants had been keeping them. Mad scientists were a given in what they did. Jon knew that. Yet he couldn't help but wonder if there was any type of mental screening the government did on scientists they recruited. Looked like they kept picking the nut jobs.

The last few months had taught Jon one thing. The people in power had lost control a long time ago. Maybe they never even had it. He could still vividly remember the fear in the eyes of the scientists who had helped to make him what he was now.

A killing machine.

Half-man, half-tiger. All killer.

Lukian's mate, Peren, was the daughter of one of the men who had taken over the experiments. He'd not been the founder of it, but had been who helped to perfect the creation of the team. He didn't fear them. But others who worked on the project before him did. They'd seen the horrors of it. They'd seen men who had volunteered to be all they could be die horrible deaths. Setting aside Lukian, they'd all been humans with supernatural traits somewhere in their family ancestry. Most were so faint it was barely there but it had been enough. Enough for the scientists to be able to try to build from. But it hadn't worked as planned. Some took to it. Some they watched go mad. And they watched others become hardened killers.

Jon remained silent in the SUV, wanting to encourage his brothers to simply break away, go it on their own from here on out. They never would. They were that loyal to their country. Problem was, their country wasn't in any way loyal to them.

Case in point, they were breaking up the team, even temporarily, and possibly sending another I-Op to his death. It was hard not to be bitter. Hard not to let it all get to him. He knew his emotions were all over the place and, as of late, finding a dark place to reside. He worried that he was like Parker—one of the broken test subjects.

All Jon had holding him together was his teammates. He knew that. He just wished the higher-ups did too.

"Hey, you still with us?" asked Eadan, bringing Jon's attention to him.

"Yeah. Sorry."

"Daydreaming about hot chicks?" Wilson questioned, grinning like a fool.

Jon's lips twitched as he tried not to laugh. "And then some."

Wilson batted his lashes in an over-the-top manner. "Describe them to us. We're all mated and aren't allowed to daydream about any women other than our wives."

Eadan shook his head. "Don't count me in that mix. I'm single."

"For now," warned Wilson. "You heard Green. Your sister keeps talking like it won't be much longer before you meet your mate."

Green laughed over their comms. "Mel is convinced it's going to happen very soon."

Jon just hoped when it came to his fate Melanie kept her faerie future-reading powers to herself. He looked to Eadan. "Try not to leak anything on me, okay?"

Eadan laughed. "I'll do my best."

TWO

EADAN SAT in one of the back rooms at Paranormal Security and Intelligence Headquarters,
reading through the briefing files on the table
before him. PSI was flashier than the I-Ops
Headquarters, which was hardly shabby. But
PSI was nearly three times the size and seemed
to like everything looking sleek and modern.
Since he'd been a member, they'd redone the
place several times. He never asked who was
paying the bills.

He probably didn't want to know.

He'd been reluctant at first when the
director of PSI had insisted he be loaned out to
the Immortal Ops Team. He'd known little of
them prior to being thrust among their ranks,

and he had to admit his first impression of them wasn't good.

Roi, in particular, had rubbed him the wrong way. Didn't help that the guy was mated to Eadan's ex-wife. His strong dislike of Roi had changed during his time with them. They'd forged a bond—they were brothers, even if not by blood. And he was happy Missy found happiness. He and Missy weren't mates. He understood that.

Though Roi was still a dick. Didn't help he was a werewolf. Tended to make his mood volatile on a good day. Eadan spent enough time around shifters to learn the differences in how they reacted, how they fought and how they calmed down. Werewolves were often the worst to bring back from the brink of rage. Although it often took the most to get them into a blood rage. That, at least, was something.

As he leafed through the files about the Asia Project, he pulled focus, concentrating on what was before him. Some of the intel regarding the project was fuzzy at best. From what Intel had been able to gather over twenty years ago, DNA splicing and manipulation techniques were done to babies in utero. Their mothers were never seen or heard from again. The children of this horrendous project had been gathered by the masterminds and placed in various orphanages around the world. Try as they might, those seeking to help the children were unable to track them. All they knew was they were out there, aging, coming into their supernatural gifts and going through only the goddess knew what.

PSI was in possession of two lists of names taken from the enemy. From what they could gather, the names on the list he was currently reading belonged to those who had been subjected to testing during the Asia Project.

He'd been given a brief glimpse of the lists when they'd first come to light, but this was the first time he'd been granted unlimited access to it all. He'd understood the lists were long, but he'd not realized that behind each name were directives. Some said to retrieve. Others said retrieve or eliminate. A rare few simply said eliminate.

"Even after everything these people have lived through, it comes to this?" he asked. He read onward and his stomach dropped. "Wait, Intel is now telling us the Asia Project never stopped? Are they certain?"

"Yes. What are your thoughts?" asked General Jack C. Newman, the director of PSI, as he entered the room. The werelion had been Eadan's father-in-law at one point. Now he was just his boss and friend.

"My thoughts are I'm about to be sick," he replied and he was. He knew the I-Ops weren't exactly created by way of cute kittens and fluffy bunnies, but the shit he'd read about the Asia Project nearly cost him his lunch. The things they did to those children, those babies. Only the sickest monsters in the world could behave in such a way.

The general nodded. "I had the same reaction."

Jack pushed the second list in Eadan's direction and Eadan felt as if something else took hold of him, demanding he snatch the list from the director. He did. He wasn't sure what he was looking for, he just knew he had to look. He read down the list of names and stopped on the name Inara Nash. His forefinger stroked the name without him meaning to.

It suddenly felt hot in the briefing room.

Eadan grabbed the pitcher of water on the table and poured himself a glass. He gulped it down, his gaze never leaving the list with the name Inara Nash upon it. Drops of perspiration made their way down his back. Why was it so damn hot in the room all of a sudden?

Jack watched his actions carefully.

Eadan stared up at the man. "You wanted me to see that list. Why?"

"Any name in particular stick out to you?" asked Jack nonchalantly.

"No games," Eadan said sternly. "There are lives at stake."

"Inara Nash," Jack said. "Next to her name, what does it say?"

Eadan referred to the list again. To the right of her name was retrieve or eliminate. The entire list had sickened him. Seeing this name in particular made his insides twist into knots, but he wasn't sure why. He didn't know her. Yet it bothered him more than if he had spotted his own name on there.

"Who is she?" he asked, utterly still. He clamped his teeth, his jaw tight, tension filling his body. He knew the answer to his own question. It was there, just out of his mind's reach.

So close.

But untouchable to him just yet.

Jack held another file out for him. "This is some of the information Missy collected. What she'd hidden on a microchip until she could find the I-Ops."

Eadan remembered what had happened. He also knew the intel nearly cost Missy her life. He took the file and opened it. Pictures fell out onto the tabletop. His chest tightened to the point of near bursting. He couldn't draw in air as he looked at the surveillance shots of Inara.

She was stunning. Her long dark hair was silky and hung almost to her waist. Several of the pictures were in full color, and when he looked into her brilliantly green eyes, he couldn't stop himself from touching the photograph. He knew his behavior wasn't normal. He couldn't stop himself. Worse yet, his cock took an interest in the woman as well. It hardened, pulling at the confines of his jeans, wanting free.

More to the point, it wanted in Inara.

The pictures showed her in various locations, mostly all outside in large cities. She also looked younger than the file claimed she was. He nearly breathed a sigh of relief when he saw that she was, in fact, legal. "She's twenty-three?"

The general nodded. "According to the records we were able to find."

With a frustrated grunt, Eadan moved around the shockingly small amount of paperwork on her. "Not much then, I see."

He wanted details. Lots of them. The files before him provided little.

"No. She's managed to stay under the radar for the last six years. At least until recently." Jack touched the recent photos of her, and Eadan held back the urge to smack the photo from his grip. No one was to touch her. No one but him. "Hard to believe she's one of the children from the Asia Project, isn't it? Seems like it happened only yesterday."

Eadan didn't remind him that his own adoptive daughter had been part of that very project and was now someone's wife and a soon-to-be mother of twins. "Yeah. I'm curious, how did you piece it together?"

"She was caught on a surveillance camera, and was clearly more than human. A team was sent to gather more information about her but she managed to lose them."

That caught his attention. Losing a PSI team wasn't easy to do. It took more than luck.

It took skill and training. Training only a fellow operative could provide.

Jack eyed him warily, then glanced away quickly. "Not once, but three times."

"Three times? How?" Eadan asked in stunned disbelief. She wasn't an operative. And she wasn't a Shadow Agent. Even though they operated off the grid, Eadan had been made aware of who they were because he was a special kind of handler. One who had the trust of the director.

He lifted the photograph Jack was so interested in. The woman was outside a building that had a sign on it.

West Street Shelter.

He didn't need to be told it was a homeless shelter. The forlorn look on her beautiful face, the dark circles under her eyes, the clothes that didn't fit her right and looking thinner than she should. She was on the streets.

The knowledge struck him in the solar plexus. He'd have doubled over if he wasn't already seated. Instead, he used the table and gripped it tight, taking slow, measured breaths.

"Exactly," Jack stated, sadness lacing his voice. "We pulled a partial print and were able to find information on her from six years ago. Then nothing. What we did find was interesting. It left little doubt in our minds that she's from the Asia Project."

"Any word on where she is now?" There was no hiding the desperation in his voice so he didn't bother trying.

The pensive look on Jack's face worried Eadan. "In Helmuth's territory."

"The dick who controls the paranormal underground in Seattle?"

Jack nodded. "The very same. And it gets worse. Helmuth has now been linked to both Krauss and Molyneux."

It was bad enough Krauss had big-time supporters. Adding in Helmuth didn't help matters. Seemed like the whole of the paranormal bad-guy community was gathering together and setting aside differences for an end game Eadan wasn't sure he wanted to learn about.

"Why not send the I-Ops on this?" he asked. It was a legitimate question. They'd been following Krauss around, trying to get a handle on his next move, for months. They were the likely choice. The Asia Project was, for lack of a better word, their baby.

Jack took a seat. While immortal, Jack was very old for a shifter, so much so that he now looked to be middle-aged. It took a long time for a shifter to get to that point. Jack wore his age around the eyes, as if he'd seen too much in his long life. "Eadan, look at all the photos of her."

Eadan skimmed through them and came to a grinding halt when he spotted one with Inara drawing. Someone had taken the picture from behind her, and when Eadan looked at the sketchpad before her on the diner table, he understood why. She'd sketched him.

"That's me," he whispered, holding the photo tighter to him as if it were a lifeline to the woman. His gaze went to her hand, the one holding the pencil. He wanted to be there next to her, holding her hand, kissing it.

You don't even know her. Enough, he chastised himself. This wasn't like him. Eadan was level-headed and he never made a habit of blindly falling for a woman. Yet he felt himself tumbling fast for this one.

Jack moved that photo aside and pushed two others before him. These were also of Inara drawing. Though, she wasn't in a diner in them. The pictures were different but the subject was still the same.

He looked up at Jack. "She draws me? How? We've never met."

Jack sighed, appearing tired. "Eadan, from what we could piece together about the testing done on her, she's carrying a fair amount of werewolf DNA in her. But there is so much other introduced feline shifter DNA that we don't think she can actually shift forms." A dramatic pause followed. "There is more."

Eadan wasn't sure he wanted to hear the rest, but he needed to. "Yes?"

"From the fragmented testing results we were able to recover from the original laboratories, Inara, like all the children in the project, started out with some supernatural base, be it small or large. Inara had Fae in her. Small, but there. Our scientists are guessing one of her grandparents was the product of a Fae and human pairing. Mind you, the files were damaged. The original scientists tried to burn the evidence. We were able to forensically piece back together a portion of it. Not all."

Staring from Jack to the pictures of Inara

drawing him, Eadan began to feel as if he were falling down a rabbit hole. Nothing he was looking at made sense. Not to mention his emotions were all over the place. He'd not had this much trouble with them in years. "Say it."

Jack eased closer to him. "Eadan, you and Missy weren't true mates. You know it, I know it, everyone does."

Nodding, Eadan sat perfectly still, already guessing what was coming. "Yes. And while we'll always be friends, we're not in love with each other. She's with Roi. I get and respect that. I want her happy and I would never try to interfere with that."

"I know. She found her true mate," Jack continued. "And our people, putting together all this information before us, think this young woman here might be yours. Before you protest, I called your father in on this and asked him his thoughts. You know he's high up in the Fae world. He agrees, Eadan. He thinks Inara is your life mate."

There had to be more to the story. Eadan eyed Jack carefully. "What aren't you telling me?"

With a long, slow breath, Jack kept going.

"Before everything hit the fan here at PSI, before the rogue problems came to light, I was contacted by an ex-PSI agent. The who isn't important now. What *is* was that he was calling to tell me he thought he'd found your mate. He wouldn't say why, but Eadan, regardless of how or why he left PSI, I trust him."

"Why didn't you tell me?"

"Everything went south here. I needed your focus on PSI. Not elsewhere. It was self-ish, I know, and at the time she wasn't in danger," he said. "Honestly, I'm still pissed that you and Missy lied to me about having a rela-tionship. But you deserve more than my hurt feelings and anger. You deserve to be happy, and if intel is right, your mate is in grave danger."

Something wasn't sitting well with Eadan. "Who was the agent who contacted you?"

Jack was hesitant before responding, "James Hagen."

Eadan's temper flared. "He bailed on PSI almost ten years back. He got an agent killed."

"There is a lot about that mission you don't know," Jack replied softly as he lifted his hands to indicate the need to remain calm.

"I know Gus was my friend, a mentor, and James got him killed."

Jack shook his head. "According to the story you heard. I'm not getting into this now."

Eadan glanced at the photos of Inara. "What does James have to do with Inara?"

"We're not entirely sure. I can say they were spotted together more than once. Also, Hagen sent the photos of Inara drawing you." Jack met his gaze. "Some speculate he and Inara are or were lovers."

Eadan saw red. No one was to touch Inara. No one but him.

His breath caught at the realization he was ready to launch a war over a woman he didn't know. Jack watched his movements, almost as if he expected the negative reaction.

"The I-Ops could have learned all this," he said. "Why just pull me?"

"The werewolf DNA," Jack answered.

Eadan tipped his head, his anger still bristling at the surface. "I'm not following."

"It's a match for Lukian and Roi's bloodline." Jack stood and walked toward the door. He looked back. "Lukian has been alive a very long time. He's king among his kind. He views

Roi as his brother because of the bloodbond they share. Where do you think Lukian's head will be when he learns there is a young woman out there who had a parent that was half-were-wolf. Not just any werewolf, mind you, but from his line. A line he thought had no one aside from him, Roi and their soon-to-be children?"

It took Eadan a moment to follow. "You're thinking she's family to him somehow?"

Jack inclined his head. "And if she's family to Lukian…"

"She's family to Roi."

"If I had to guess, they'll see her as a little sister of sorts. You're not a shifter, but I am, and I can tell you how I'd feel. How I'd view the young woman if it were me and how I'd prob-ably do something very stupid to save her. And, Eadan, while you might not hold a lot of love for Roi, he's mated to Missy and they're expecting twins."

Eadan stood as well. "And if Roi does some-thing stupid and gets himself killed over Inara, Missy and her babies are on their own."

"Yeah." Jack touched the door handle. "For this mission, it's best you leave the I-Ops out of it. I've arranged for another PSI Op to meet you in Seattle."

"Who?"

"Duke Marlow," returned Jack.

Eadan groaned. "What is with sticking me with all the damn werewolves?"

Jack grinned. "If we're right, your soon-to-be wife counts as one."

THREE

INARA NASH MOVED through the streets of the city. The sun had set some two hours prior, taking with it her sense of security, regardless how false it was. It didn't matter if it was day or night. She wasn't safe. The sun merely changed what was chasing her, not who. The soles of her worn shoes padded along the cracked pavement. Trash lined the side of the street. At some point it would be picked up, but more would be there to take its place. The people who lived here didn't care. If she had a place to call home, she'd care. She'd tend to it.

That was just a dream. She'd never be free to settle in one place long enough to call it home. And if she was in a place too long, it would probably mean it was her grave. There were days the sound of that appealed to her. She understood how messed up that was, but it was the truth.

As a child she'd visited a few of the shops in this area with her adoptive mother, watching the woman spend money as if it really did grow on trees. Though, back then, she'd thought the woman with her was the woman who had given birth to her.

She flinched as painful memories assailed her.

You're not natural.

The words still clung to the air around her as if they were only freshly spoken. Funny the weight people's words held. They were like an albatross around her neck, there to forever remind her of what she was and wasn't.

The look in her adoptive mother's eyes when she'd said them haunted Inara to this day. They had been the last words spoken between them. Inara had taken to the streets that night. She wasn't welcome in the home she'd known as a child. That was fine. She didn't need them.

She blew out a slow breath, and because of the dropping temperature she was able to actually see it. For the briefest of moments she wished she could go back to a time when she'd press her nose to the shop windows and ask for sweet treats from her mother. The area wasn't the same inviting space it used to be. Once the area had been a prime location. The place every young and up-and-coming transplant to the city wanted to be. It was the life of the city. Gangs and crime entered and all that changed. Now the area was a place no one willingly wandered into after dark.

Well, no one but her and others like her.

The unnatural.

She walked past two women, each dressed in barely anything. One watched her and grinned. "Got a light?"

"No," she said, speeding her pace. Her mentor had taught her to avoid the hookers who frequented the paranormal hot spots. They were generally more than met the eye and tended to bring a shit storm of trouble wherever they went. She had enough on her own.

She missed Jimmy. Especially during times like this. He'd been her mentor. A freak of nature who had to make it by staying under the radar, like her. He'd helped her learn to fend for herself. Helped her spot dangers and even taught her how to spot certain supernaturals. Best part was, he taught her the ones to avoid at all cost.

Shifter. That was what Jimmy said he smelled on her when he first found her, rummaging through a trash can when she was only fifteen, looking for anything that was still edible. She thought he was nuts at first, but something deep down told her to trust him. She'd never been able to shift forms like he could, but she did possess similar skills. And a few more they tended not to talk about. They'd forged an unbreakable bond. One she missed dearly.

"Even if you're not tough—pretend. It can convince a lot of people," she murmured, thinking of Jimmy's words of wisdom. "And never lose your ability to laugh."

His lessons were words she lived by.

Damn him for getting caught. Damn him for sacrificing himself for her. She wanted to hate him for that, but she loved him too much to bother. This area was one he'd taught her about. He'd walked her through it enough times that she knew most of it like the back of her hand. However, this particular section was newer to her.

She knew supernaturals had flocked to the space. They'd taken a deep foothold within the crime community and ran things now. Like they did in so many large cities. If regulars only knew the truth. She could barely remember a time when she was ignorant of what truly lurked in the darkened recesses. It was a happy time. A time before she became a runner.

"Damn men in black."

She nearly laughed at the absurdity of it all.

Yes, she was on the run from the men in black.

Hollywood would have a field day with her. Then again, they'd have to swallow the truth that some people weren't really people at all. Some were monsters.

She was a monster of sorts. No one had been able to label her. All she knew was she was more than human, an outcast and wanted by all the wrong people. None of it made for a happy gal.

She kept walking, despite the bitter cold rain stinging her cheeks. The temperature had dropped when the sun went down and would only continue to do so as long as the rain held out. There seemed to be no end to it in sight. Keeping her head low, she avoided making eye contact with anyone. She couldn't be sure if they would remember her should anyone come looking later.

She stepped into a small alcove in the alley and put her back to the wall. Pieces of the brick flecked off and onto her shoulder. She brushed them away as best she could, considering how damp her sweatshirt was. The hoodie she wore had done little to shield her from the drizzle that had started nearly thirty minutes prior and had remained constant. If anything, the hoodie acted like a sponge. She'd be soaked to the bone soon enough.

She was happy she'd decided to stash her sketchpad and drawing materials. She didn't own much except them, and her sketchpad meant the world to her. Jimmy used to laugh at her because of the one thing she enjoyed drawing most—a man she'd never met and who wasn't real. He just sort of came to her when she had pencil in hand, and sometimes even in her dreams, if only for fleeting moments. Didn't matter. His face and his blue-gray eyes were burned into her brain. She'd even managed to sell a few of her drawings of him. She wasn't sure what the buyer did with them or why the person picked the naked ones. The money provided much needed food.

The man she drew was her guardian angel, even if he wasn't real. To her, he represented peace and serenity. She could use a little of both.

Wet, hungry and tired, she closed her eyes and let out a long breath. She needed a place to hunker down and sleep for a few days straight. Not to mention food. She needed food. Her reserve money was tapped out and she'd not been able to shake her followers for long enough intervals to work any odd jobs and make some cash.

Damn them.

She knew what she'd have to do. And she hated it. Hated that she'd been reduced to this. A twenty-three–year-old woman who had to scrape by just to survive. She knew the alley she was on dead-ended into Pierce Street. And Pierce was well-known for its underground paranormal, illegal activities. She'd made it a point to learn all she could about the area before heading to it.

Entering unfamiliar territory while men who wanted to do heavens-only-knew-what were fast on your heels wasn't smart, and she may be a lot of things but she wasn't stupid. She nearly laughed. It was that or cry, and she'd shed too many tears already. She wouldn't gift them anymore.

She leaned out, glancing down the length of the alley in both directions. Her long, dark hair fell forward as rain began to fall upon her head once more. She hated the rain anymore. When she was very little, she'd loved it. Having to live on the streets and be subjected to the elements, often without shelter, changed her views on a lot of things. Snow was no longer pretty. It meant cold and cold could mean death.

Possibly death.

She'd survived some crazy things and had wondered what, if anything, could actually kill her. She didn't want to find out.

Night always brought a new set of challenges. It wasn't bad enough she was hunted during the day, she had to be hunted even more so at night.

The vamps mixes—that was what came for her in the dark. They were the worst. The cold empty eyes, the lightning-fast speed and the smell. It was unlike anything she'd ever smelled before. That was what normally gave the evil ones away.

Their stench.

Had anyone told her ten years ago she'd be on the run from all sorts of supernaturals, she'd have laughed in their faces. The things that came for her were relentless. She'd been lucky so far, always getting away even if just barely.

A sinking feeling came over. Her luck was running out. She knew it. Felt it in her bones.

Reaching into her jeans pocket, she shivered slightly as she withdrew a crumpled, damp piece of paper. Despair sank to the pit of her stomach. The address was close. She looked to the warehouse at the end of the alley.

She'd get in and get out as fast as she could. These types of underground fight clubs lasted at most a week in one area. If she didn't get in there tonight, she'd miss her chance and would have to hunt down information on the next one. A red X on the side of the door with a dot on both sides meant she was in the right place. She just needed to grab some money and possibly some food. Stealing from scumbags didn't bother her. It's why she dared to come here. Nothing but the bad element was here. She'd have no guilt later and she needed food and a roof over her head. She couldn't stay in one place long enough to do anything even close to honest work. It was this or go hungry.

She rounded the corner, knowing a back exit would be used for the event. A big guy wearing a leather jacket and sunglasses was there. She pursed her lips at the sight of him. Really? Sunglasses at night?

"You have got to be kidding me," she mouthed as she approached him. He gave her a quick look over as if to dare her to try to gain entrance through him. She lifted her chin to him but kept on going.

She wasn't strong enough to deal with him right now. Under better circumstances she could handle a guy like him. Right now, she could barely keep herself upright. Picking a fight with a big shifter wasn't smart. Maybe later, after she had some food.

Or I could just let someone bigger and better pick a fight with the guy. And there was always someone bigger and better. She'd learned that along the way. Jimmy was proof of that. In her mind he'd been invincible. That hadn't been the reality.

They'd gotten him. And they most certainly would have killed him. He was simply too powerful to allow to live. She understood the way of it. Well, most of it anyways.

She still couldn't understand why the hell she was so important to the men in black. There were endless amounts of supernaturals to pick from. What was special about her? She'd seen all of what Jimmy could do and she couldn't hold a candle to the man. She couldn't shapeshift like he could.

Jimmy had known but hadn't said. He'd pretend he had no clue, but she'd learned to read his face. She knew his tells. And he most certainly knew what they wanted with her but had never felt the need to clue her in on it.

Inara slinked down the side of the warehouse, moving beyond the bouncer's line of sight. He wouldn't hear her. Not with the magic coating the area, blocking the majority of noise. She found a rolling dumpster and neared it. The stench coming from it nearly chased her away. She couldn't be certain, but it smelled like a dead body was in it. With the crowd gathered inside, she wouldn't put it past them. These fights tended to be death matches. That meant the bodies did pile up.

Her stomach did a few flip-flops before she was able to even touch the trashcan. It was on wheels and rolled with relative ease. The smell only intensified. She thought she might actually find a corpse or two there. Nothing but rotting garbage littered the area. The smell intensified as she bent near some boxes of old Thai food. Covering her nose, Inara leaned away as she used her free hand to check the metal panels of the building. It took four tries but she found one that wasn't secured. She yanked on it and looked in. She spotted feet and legs far enough off in the distance that it didn't appear as though anyone would notice her entering.

Perfect.

Crawling in, she held her breath, hoping no one would see her in the act. What aided her in keeping other shifters from hearing her also hindered her. If there was anyone near, she wouldn't hear them either.

Rust from the panel she held smeared onto her hands. Jimmy had sworn up and down she wasn't susceptible to human diseases. Tetanus didn't sound pleasant. She hoped he was right. The very idea she'd managed to stay alive all these years, only to go out by way of a rusty panel, didn't sit well with her.

Once inside she replaced the panel and turned, surveying the situation. She was instantly hit with the sounds and smells of hundreds of people packed into the place. She'd not heard anything from outside, but that was common in these types of fights. The spells she knew the event organizers used to hide the warehouse's true purpose were strong. Stronger than others she'd crossed.

Since she'd been on the streets, she'd been to too many of these underground fights to count. Often, Jimmy would fight in them, earning extra money for them. Other times, when Jimmy hadn't been with her, she'd learned to sneak around and steal what she needed to get by. It wasn't a life she was proud of, but it was the hand she'd been dealt.

Sometimes, you did things you never thought you would in order to live.

The fight clubs were meccas for the weird, wacky and wanting-to-die supernaturals. Seemed like shifters more than any other paranormal species flocked to the fights. They had a lot of bottled-up testosterone, so it made sense. Most vampires she'd met were manipulative and up to no good. Made sense they'd show too. She only hoped they weren't evil through and through or their smell would turn her stomach the entire length of the event.

At least they didn't make her sneeze like magiks did. She really disliked magiks. For one, their scent always made her sneeze, and for two, the ones she'd bumped into were even more manipulative than the vampires. And that was damn hard to be.

So long as there were no signs of the men chasing her, she'd deal with whatever came. Deep down in her gut, her senses began to churn, alerting her to something being off. She sniffed the air, drawing in the scent of vampires. A lot of them. More than she'd smelled in one location ever. They didn't tend to come in groups. They seemed to be more solitary in their habits. Unless they were working toward a very bad common goal.

Keep your head down. Get some cash and get out, she repeated in her head again and again.

She snuck past a group of men and darted

down an unmanned area, walking down the dimly lit corridor. Now that she was inside, the wards keeping those passing by the warehouse from hearing what was going on inside were gone. She could hear other women talking. Her heightened sense of hearing permitted her to often hear more than she wanted to. It had first started when she was a child, and it had scared and overwhelmed her. She'd heard every voice around her. The tick of every clock. The beat of every heart. She'd curled into a tiny ball and cried. Her adoptive parents took her to a special doctor.

Looking back, Inara had doubts even then about the doctor and her adoptive parents. There were always shady glances, conversations taking place far from her, and back-room dealings. Something had been off, but she'd not pieced it all together.

"You look like a tramp," a girl said to another, the voice carrying down the corridor, pulling Inara from her memories of the past. "We're supposed to look hot, not like skanks."

"Bitch, I know you're not talking to me," another girl returned.

"Should you refer to me as a bitch again,

there won't be enough of you left for the people here to piece back together," the first returned, sounding calm, as though she had years and wisdom on her side.

Inara steeled herself as she moved back the dingy curtain to the ring girl area. The curtain smelled of smoke and sex. She didn't want to know what it used to be. Probably a bedspread in a seedy hotel. She moved past it quickly, wanting it away from her as fast as possible. She collided with a woman and stepped back, catching the woman before she fell. The woman wore a barely-there dress and a fur coat, of all things. Diamonds worth more than Inara wanted to take a guess at adorned the woman's ears and neck. Everything about her said she had money and lots of it.

What the hell was she doing behind the curtain for the ring girls? Women like her didn't frequent dives like this unless they were on the arms of rich high rollers. Maybe she was lost.

Within seconds Inara was sneezing. A sure sign the woman was a magik. Of course she was. Probably meant she couldn't be trusted too.

The woman's dark eyes narrowed on her. "You should watch where you are going."

Inara simply stared at her. "Sorry."

Whatever the woman saw when looking at Inara must have warned her off of starting anything. She nodded. "Be more careful."

"Sure thing." Inara sneezed again. She was going to leave well enough alone but her stomach began to growl loudly. "Hey, they have any food anywhere?"

Pity slipped over the woman's eyes. "Oh, sugar, you're a street rat, aren't you?"

She'd become familiar with the term years ago and inclined her head. "Just need some food, then I'll be on my way."

The redhead put her hand on Inara's shoulder and Inara stiffened. "Come on. I've got some food in the back. I bring plenty for my girls. That one over there with the loud mouth is Candy." The redhead paused. "And if she continues with the attitude, she will be in far worse shape than you are."

Inara said nothing as a blonde with too much makeup on finished tying the top of her bikini up. The blonde pressed a smile to her face and picked up a Round One sign. "Don't mind me, I'm just working for a living."

Inara considering punching the bitch. She

resisted. Plus, she wasn't exactly up to it at the moment.

The redhead sighed. "Some girls are lost causes. But enough of Candy. Let's get you cleaned up and fed."

"I'm good. Thank you."

The woman's lips pursed. "You don't trust me."

Inara said nothing. She'd learned not to trust magiks. It was nothing against the redhead in particular. Just magiks in general.

"The food is back there. I'll stay out here if it makes you feel better."

It did.

"I was a street rat once too," the woman returned. "That was a long, long time ago but I remember what it was like. I wouldn't wish the life on anyone. Got a name?"

Inara stood there staring at her. She wasn't about to give this stranger her name.

The redhead smiled more. "I'm Jinx."

Jinx?

Jimmy had spoken of Jinx. More than once. The way he talked about her made her sound like a modern-day madam with connections that ran deep in the paranormal underground. He also talked about trusting her.

"I'm Inara."

Jinx gasped and leaned in close, whispering, "Jimmy's charge?"

She managed a nod.

Jinx glanced around, looking almost frantic for a moment. "You shouldn't be here."

"I know."

"Oh, for the love of cock, tell me you're not here to rob the betting money." She shook her head. "Forget it. I know Jimmy and I know what he taught you. You're here for the money."

"And food," Inara offered with a grin that faded quickly.

"Where is Jimmy? I'm going to strangle him for bringing you here."

Inara stilled. "You don't know?"

"Know what?" Jinx asked.

"He was taken."

Jinx swayed and Inara had to steady her. "When?" the woman asked.

"Months ago."

"And you've been on your own since then?"

"I get by," Inara protested.

Jinx pursed her lips. "Oh yes, I see. Come on. I've got some fruit and snacks in the back." She led Inara to a back room and handed her an apple, a banana and a granola bar. Without really stopping to chew, Inara had the granola bar scarfed down within a minute. The redhead looked saddened as she pushed Inara's dark hair behind her ear.

Inara peeled the banana, unconcerned with the mess she was making. "Thanks for the food."

Something on Jinx's expression changed. Her face went from saddened to fearful. "Listen, go that room over there. You'll find water bottles and a wash room."

"Thank you," she said as another sneeze followed. It would end soon enough, but in the meantime she was in hell and they didn't offer an over-the-counter tablet for her problem.

FOUR

EADAN GLANCED around the dark alleyway, sure he'd taken a wrong turn somewhere. This was the great lead Jack had? Dammit, he had to find Inara. The flight here felt at least ten times longer than it actually had been. Hearing he had a potential mate and that she was in danger was a hell of a motivating factor.

So far, there had been no sign of Inara and no sign of Duke Marlow. Eadan had given up waiting on backup and decided to go it alone. Duke would have to catch up with him later. Inara needed him now and he wouldn't let anything happen to her. Didn't matter that they'd never met. Simply seeing her photo had done him in. She was his. He felt it deep down in his bones. And his magik tingled at the idea of taking her, claiming her as his life mate.

He just had to find her first.

He continued down the alley. So far, he'd spotted a passed-out older man who had wet his pants and was hugging an empty bottle of cheap wine as he whispered sweet nothings to it in his state of drunkenness, several women selling themselves to what he could only guess was the lowest bidder, and two assholes fighting over a car, but no sign of the girl from the photograph.

Damn Krauss, Molyneux and Helmuth. Damn them all to hell. It was because of men like them that there had been so much death and destruction. The quest for everlasting life, for ultimate power and for super soldiers was going to doom them all.

If it hadn't already.

He didn't understand the craze to invent or "improve" upon existing supernaturals or natural-born gifts. Eadan came by his supernatural gifts honestly. He was a born Fae. Both his parents were full-blooded Fae as well. Hell, they were considered noble within the Fae world.

That was a good and bad thing. Good because it gave him pull and rank within the Fae community. Bad because he'd stopped ageing in his early twenties, forever locked into a baby face. What was worse, every time he tried to cut his hair it only grew back. Sometimes by the next morning.

It was hard to look like a badass next to a bunch of shifter-ops when he was cursed with long, blond hair and a face that at best grew a small dusting of facial hair. Roi gave him the hardest time. The other guys just laughed. Eadan knew it was all in fun. Even though he did wish he could pull off the rugged look.

He doubted that would happen. His father was centuries old and still looked fresh faced and barely thirty. The odds were not in Eadan's favor.

Could have been worse. He'd seen some interesting creatures that spawned from the Fae community. Things that could never live in the open because it was impossible for them to blend as humans. Some should be feared. Others were feared but had hearts of gold. In the end, it didn't matter. They couldn't expose humans to what was truly out there. There would be chaos.

A complete meltdown of society.

A lot of what was running around the super-natural underground was a mix of things. At one point it was all born that way. Not anymore. Now, thanks to the mad scientist Krauss, there were hodgepodges of paranormal on the loose and worse.

If that wasn't bad enough, PSI had had a surge of traitors within the last year, something it hadn't had in decades. Hell, most of the oper-atives within the organization were pushing a century, if not older. They tended to learn from their mistakes and to avoid allowing history to repeat itself. Eadan wasn't sure what the fuck had happened within PSI, but it had gone to hell fast and was hopefully on the mend. He hadn't had much of a chance to ask about it when he met with the general. Jack was all busi-ness and insistent Eadan get his butt in gear and get out here as quick as he could. Apparently, intel had surfaced on an Asia Project subject being in the area.

He had half a mind to phone headquarters

and ask if Intel had started smoking something funny. He'd probably get Nancy. She was one of the phone operators for PSI. She'd just as soon tell you to go fuck yourself than pass you along to the person you needed to speak with. She'd been permanently seventy-something since he could first remember meeting her twelve years prior. Rumor was, she'd been "that age" for a very long time.

Dammit, things had taken a turn for the worse with intel since he and Missy were no longer active in the organization. They'd been a force to be reckoned with, for sure. But times had changed.

He'd seek out some trusted contacts soon enough and find out what was really happening within the organization. For now, he'd do as instructed. He couldn't go to Missy for help. She wasn't a player anymore. She was going to be a mom and would more than likely never be an active agent again. The job was simply too deadly. And she'd already lost one child from it. Eadan knew she'd never risk another.

There had been a point in his life when thinking of Missy, their past marriage and their loss had been too much for him. A time when he thought he'd never move on. His sister had fixed that, taking some of the hurt and the pain from him mystically. It wasn't a fix he'd have used on himself, but it was fix he'd needed all the same. He'd become bitter and had lost his love for life. Without his sister Melanie intervening, Eadan knew he'd have spiraled out of control. Some of the sting of it all was easier to swallow knowing Missy had never been his true mate. She belonged to Roi.

That was a bitter pill to swallow.

Even now, with the help of Melanie's spell, he still had a pang of guilt, of pain that crept up on him. He focused on the task at hand, knowing he couldn't let himself slip into a funk again. He'd throw himself into work, like he always did.

The current location didn't appear to be much more than an abandoned warehouse. Looked like it would be another intel dud. He'd had a late flight in and no time to rest before he'd met with a rendezvous contact who handed him the new details. Somehow, Eadan didn't think Krauss or his accomplices would be holed up in a warehouse that looked like it could blow over in a hard wind. Stranger shit had happened, so he didn't walk away like he thought he should. The longer he remained, the more he realized something was off.

The alley was quiet. Too quiet in actuality. His brow crinkled as he looked around more, suddenly noticing the lack of anything—sounds, people, animals, city noise.

Letting his power up slowly, he stood in place, using his power to feel around him. It was then he sensed it. Additional power. Old and powerful.

Interesting.

Deciding it warranted a closer look, Eadan went around to the side of the warehouse. One rather large man stood there. He looked like he enjoyed too much fast food to be able to do much in the way of damage. Unless he planned to attack Eadan with his cholesterol. As Eadan approached him, the man postured as if his sheer size would scare Eadan away.

Eadan nearly laughed. He'd seen bigger and badder.

"What's the word?" the man demanded, hands up, shoulders back. He looked ridiculous. If Eadan had to guess, he'd say the guy was a shifter of some sort—though he wasn't alpha. He was just pretending to be.

Drawing up his magik more, Eadan merely smiled. "You will permit me entrance." There was a push to his voice. One he knew even supernaturals would have difficultly ignoring. It was why he made a good Shadow Agent. He didn't generally need anyone else with him. Though, he had to admit he missed his new "brothers." Roi would have punched his way into the warehouse. Wilson would have probably fallen through the roof by mistake. Jon would have watched it from a distance, through a scope on his sniper rifle, and Lukian would have simply raised a brow and demanded to be permitted in—no magik to his cause. Green was a different kind of Op. One who had surprised them all with a badass side. He'd probably concoct a potion to put the bouncer to sleep. That seemed like a science geek thing to do.

Green took some getting used to. Technically, he was Eadan's brother-in-law now that he was mated to Melanie, Eadan's only sibling. The man needed a medal for that. Melanie was a handful during the best of times. He couldn't imagine any guy wanting to spend eternity with her.

Eadan waited as his magik trickled over the guy at the entrance. The bouncer nodded and stepped aside. Eadan couldn't stop himself as he leaned and continued to push power over the man. "And the new entrance phrase is, you're a dick."

The man nodded. "I'm a dick."

With a snort, Eadan continued into the warehouse. Sometimes being magik was way too fun.

The minute he fully crossed the threshold, the silence that had been outside vanished, replaced by loud pulsating music and an even louder crowd of people all gathered around something in the center. He pushed his way through the throng of sweaty bodies only to emerge near a ring set up in the center.

When he spotted the black skull flag erected at two points near the edges of the ring, he understood fully what he'd stumbled upon. An illegal underground fight ring. One that no doubt catered to the supernatural but wasn't sanctioned. He'd attended several in his life. Each was seedier than the next and none ever led to anything good. Most were frequented by supernatural lowlifes out to make a fast buck. But in the end Eadan understood the fights had wealthy backers and connections in places good people just didn't end up.

There had been a rash of people vanishing who had been associated with the fights and the lifestyle. If Krauss and Molyneux and whoever the hell else they were in bed with had their hands in this too, then Eadan wasn't surprised. They were synonymous with problems. What Eadan couldn't wrap his mind around was why the general had sent him alone. If this did tie back to Krauss, then why not include the I-Ops?

Nothing made sense.

All he was sure of was the warehouse smelled like sweat and beer.

A leggy blonde girl held up a sign with the number two on it. The bikini she wore barely covered anything. There was a time she might have been hot, but she looked like she'd been ridden hard. Life hadn't been kind to that one.

The men around him whistled and carried on like fools, each shouting disgusting things at the woman. She smiled and walked with more of a sway to her hips. Shaking his head, Eadan pulled his focus from her and onto the men in the corners of the ring. Cautiously, he let his magik up enough to scan them, but ran into a bit of resistance. That was strange. Sure, the power he'd sensed before entering was old and powerful, but Eadan was no magikal light-weight. Far from it. Yet he had to strain to do a task that would normally be second nature.

"Show it off, Candy!" a man shouted to the woman in the ring.

Eadan kept going, making his way past the ring area, toward the behind the scenes area. It took more magik than it should have to get the guys guarding the area to turn and look away at the same time. When they did, Eadan strolled through the corridor. The stench of the ware-house lifted. He continued on, curious as to why he'd been led in this direction. Two of the rooms he walked by had open doors. In one he saw a guy getting a blowjob from not one but two women, and in the other he watched men sitting around a table, snorting something or other.

Whatever it was had to be stronger than drugs you could get on the street. Those did nothing for a supernatural.

As Eadan neared the last room, he found its door closed. The urge to enter nearly consumed him. Putting his hand to the doorknob, he hesitated, listening with both his ears and his magik for what might be behind it. He heard nothing that gave him concern. He twisted the knob and opened the door slowly.

There she was. Inara, standing, naked from the waist up, her back to him, her front to an old sink basin. She covered herself from his view, her brilliantly green gaze staring wide at him in the mirror reflection. His mind said turn around and give her privacy. The rest of him forgot to take direction from his brain and remained in place.

He'd thought his reaction to her picture was strong. Seeing her in the flesh—a whole lot of flesh—nearly took him to his knees.

Air seemed to be resistant to entering his lungs. But the blood sure pooled to his cock, hardening it, making his entire body alive with desire and raw need.

Her lips were full and slightly opened in a gasp. "Holy shit! You're real?"

He couldn't seem to form a sentence to save his life. He merely nodded.

She yanked an old t-shirt over her head and spun around, her look of surprise turning to annoyance. "Knock much, ass——" She launched into a sneezing fit. When she stopped, she blinked up at him. "Ah crap, a magik?"

She sneezed again.

"W-what?"

FIVE

INARA GLARED at the blond guy who had barged in on her. He just stood there, managing to look sexy and clueless all at once. Normally, she'd have been pissed. She found herself struggling to stay in character to appear mad. She actually wanted to run and touch him, make sure she wasn't dreaming and he was really there.

More important, she wanted to feel his lips on hers.

His lips on mine? What the hell? Stop. Stranger danger, stupid.

Except he wasn't a stranger to her. Not really. She'd "known" him all her life. Her sketchpad was littered with drawings of him. She saw him when she closed her eyes at night and she'd see him when the times got really hard. His image would come to mind and just make her feel more at ease. She thought she'd invented some sort of guardian angel in her mind. Having him standing before her said otherwise.

The man was tall. Pushing six foot three or better. While he had a slender build he was toned, sinewy, like he was a badass without the bulk. His eyes were burned into her memory. Blue-gray. And his lips. Full. Sensual. As if tempting her to run over and kiss them.

She nearly did.

The hair. It was unlike any she'd seen on a guy. Long, but pulled back, and white-blond. She knew a lot of women who would kill for hair like that. Somehow, even with the hair, the guy screamed masculine. Yes, he was certainly all male. As she raked her gaze over his fitted black shirt and dark jeans, she found herself focusing on his groin. From the looks of it, seeing her topless had pleased him.

Greatly.

Heat flashed over her. She took a small step back and eyed him more. "W-who are you?

How is it I've seen you in my head? And what do you want?"

He seemed to watch her silently for what felt like hours. It was more like seconds. "You."

She blinked several times, sure she'd heard him wrong. "What?"

"I want you," he said, as if in a trance. He shook his head. "I'm here for you. To take you back to PSI."

And your luck just ran out, she thought quickly.

Alarm bells went off. Sexy guy was part of the men in black? A fit of sneezing hit her again. Dammit. She'd do that for a few more minutes at least, until she was used to his scent.

She looked back at him in time to see two men sneaking up behind him. While her brain said let them have him and run, her heart wasn't agreeing. It had no place in the argument, but hell if it wasn't winning the debate. She was connected to this man somehow. She understood that much. And while she didn't know if he was trustworthy or not, she knew she didn't want him hurt. Plus, the lips on lips thought was still weighing on her.

"Behind you!" she managed, just as they rammed an electric rod into his back and sent enough jolts through him to make his entire body flail as he crashed to the floor.

Somehow, he managed to get to his feet at an insane rate of speed. He caught the fist of one of the men and held it, looking almost amused at their attempts at taking him down. He kicked out at another, his long, muscular legs connecting with their target. He made fighting look like a sensual dance, rather than a dirty street brawl.

A third man rushed through the open door. Inara reacted, grabbing an apple from the bowl of fruit and throwing it. Her aim was true and she threw with more force than she thought she had in her. The apple hit its mark—the man's forehead. He went down hard.

Mr. Sketchpad-come-to-life glanced at the downed man and her, his eyes widening. He blocked another punch and twisted, catching the electric prod with one hand and head-butting the man holding the rod out. He twisted the rod and used it against the man, sending him flying backward into the hallway. Additional men converged on them and Inara found herself darting forward to assist.

She wasn't exactly helpless. Jimmy had

taught her things and others just came naturally. She was about to jump onto the back of one of the attackers when another rammed the electric prod he was holding into her side. She couldn't stop the scream that tore free from her.

The man from her drawings looked to her, worry on his face. It cost him dearly as three men rammed rods into him, sending so much power through him that he had to be dead.

Panic swept through her. She rushed at him, never thinking about the men with the electric rod. They tapped her with it and extreme pain followed by darkness was all she felt.

Inara came to, unsure how much time had passed. She had the feeling she'd been out a while from the way her body ached. Not to mention she was now starving again and should have been fuller from the fruit and granola bar she'd downed.

Darkness surrounded her. For a moment, she worried she'd lost her sight. It took her a second to realize the room she was in was dark. Almost too dark to see. As her eyes adjusted, she could make out metal walls with grooves in them. The more she saw the more she realized she was in a container and she wasn't alone.

Blond guy!

He was slumped against the back corner. He looked as if the two thugs had taken turns beating the shit out of him while he was out cold. Her heart thumped madly in her chest as she raced over to him. A thick chain connected from one wrist shackle to the next on him.

She'd not been shackled.

Why?

And who had them?

It took her a bit to gather her emotions and concentrate on what was happening. She touched the man's head and came away with blood from near his temple. She stiffened. He was real. She couldn't get over the knowledge. For so long he'd been her private thought—her way to cope with any situation. All along he was a real person. She didn't understand why his image was burned into her brain or why she'd been compelled to put his face to paper. The strangest part was how protective of the drawings she was. They were hers and no one was allowed to touch them.

Ever.

Thankfully, they were still hidden away.

You have the real thing lying before you.

And she did. She touched him again, this time on his upper chest. Hot damn, the man was rock hard. Closing her eyes tight, she swallowed hard, trying to get herself to think about anything other than sex. She was locked in a container that looked like something that would be pulled by a train, and she was thinking about sex.

Look at him and try not to think about it.

Dammit. Her inner voice was annoying. In its defense, he was exceptionally good looking. She'd seen runway models who were uglier. And the hair. So much of it. She wondered what it would be like if he was above her, his hair falling down, framing them in an intimate moment.

Kiss him now. He'll never know.

She grunted and chastised her inner voice for being a creepy pervert.

Her inner thighs tingled with excitement. Right be damned. The man who was literally from her dreams was before her. She traced her hand over his chest more. Did he have any fat on him? As Inara's hand moved down to the top of his jeans, she had a come-to-the-gods moment and pulled it away. It was harder to do than it should have been.

He stirred.

There was a slight buzz to the air around her. For a moment, she assumed it was coming from the blond guy. When she realized it was emanating from her, she gasped and nearly pulled away from the man. The pulsing need to touch him again won out. She laid her hands on him, palms over his upper chest and the buzz around her grew. It consumed her arms first, moving through her torso and then downward. Gasping for breaths, she panted as she kept her hands on the man.

She blinked, sure her mind was playing tricks on her as the gash on his head closed over. The only sign there had been a cut at all was the leftover blood. She yanked her hands away from him, unsure exactly what had happened between them.

He stirred and reached out for her, catching her hands in his. She yelped. He tugged, pulling her closer. The strange buzzing intensified even more. It sounded like hundreds of bees were around them when in reality there were none to be seen.

He drew her down more, his eyes still closed, his full lips parting. Inara tried to pull free but not that hard. She was sort of pleased to be this close to him. His breath skated over her lips and she bit her inner cheek in an attempt to bring her rational mind around to thinking for her again in place of her hormones.

Sadly, her hormones won out.

This man was sexy in a way that made her ovaries scream at her to stop thinking at all and jump his bones. Alarmed by the raw need to have him, she managed to resist. It was hard.

Very hard.

Especially when he moaned her name out in a hushed whisper. The way he said it was so incredibly erotic that her nipples responded, hardening, scraping against the thin material of her t-shirt.

Shit. If he could do this to her when he was out like a light, what could he do to her awake? She nearly moaned as well at the thought. "M-Mister, please wake up before I give in and pet something you might not want me petting."

"Hmm?" he mumbled as his blue-gray eyes snapped opened. "Inara!"

"Shh, I'm right here. I'm fine." She hid her smile even though she should have been freaked he knew her name. He was awake. That had to be good. She had to tug to get her hands free from his, not that she truly wanted to be released. It just seemed like the right thing to do, considering everything.

He sat up slowly and as best he could with his hands bound, though the chain did have a good amount of give. She wondered what the purpose of it was. He could still move around. His skin, where the shackles lay, was red as if he was allergic to them.

He groaned and then shifted his weight up, sitting on his own. "What the hell happened?"

Inara had to force herself to stop staring at his lips. "You were so busy looking at my boobs that you missed the goons coming up behind you," she snapped. Kissing him was what she'd wanted to do, but somehow she only managed to get catty with him. "You had the upper hand until you worried more about me than you."

His gaze raked over her, settling on her covered chest. A silly, lopsided grin spread over his face. "Yeah, your breasts."

She nearly smacked him, but was too happy to see him sitting up on his own to bother. "We have more important things to focus on here."

"If you say so," he said, still grinning at her

chest. He shook his head slightly and then stiffened. "How long have we been in here?"

Inara debated on telling him her theory. "I think we've been here a while now."

He was quiet for a bit. "I think you're right."

"Got a name?"

"Eadan."

He brought his hands up and touched the side of his head, where the blood had pooled. "Ouch." He seemed confused, as if he was expecting an injury. She didn't comment. No sense announcing something she didn't fully understand and, really, who would believe a bunch of invisible bees showed up to save the day?

She slid even closer to him, their bodies touching. At least she'd finally stopped sneezing around him. "So, you're magik?"

He tipped his head slightly. "I am, but how did you know that?"

She touched the tip of her nose. "I seem to have an allergy to magiks. They make me sneeze."

His bright smile nearly stole her breath. Hot damn he was sexy, even beat up. "Magiks make you sneeze?"

She shrugged. "Yep."

His lopsided grin made her heart flutter. "Ironic."

"Why is that?"

"No reason. So, why does it make you sneeze?"

"Don't know why. But I end up with sneezing fits that normally last an hour or two. Once I'm used to your scent, I don't do it too much."

"I have a scent?" he questioned, as he glanced around the container they were being held in. She strongly suspected he was trying to keep her calm while he looked for a way to escape.

"You do." She sat on her bottom next to him. "Yours is different from other magiks. Yours is more of a mix of fresh air and mountaintops. I guess the best way to put it is you smell like nature."

"That a good or bad thing?" He moved to his hands and knees and struggled a bit with being shackled as he stood. She stood too, using her body to help him keep his balance. From the looks of him, the goons had not only electrocuted him and beat the crap out of him, they'd more than likely electrocuted him again for good measure.

"It's a good thing," she admitted. "What did you do to piss these guys off so much?"

He was quiet a second and she got the sense he was trying to decide if he'd be honest or lie. She really hoped he picked option one.

He stood on his own and stared down at her. Man, he was tall. She wasn't short for a woman, yet he towered over her. "I came here looking for you. I'm guessing they figured that out."

"Me?" She was about to ask why and it hit her. "You're a man in black."

His brow arched. "A who in what?"

"Man. *In black*," she answered slowly, because he probably was suffering a brain injury or something. Guess the invisa-bees hadn't been all that helpful after all.

He sighed. "I don't know what you're talking about."

"A guy from the organization that has been hunting me down for years," she said, her voice raising. "The same goons who have come for me over and over, trying to toss me in an unmarked van?"

He snorted.

"I don't find that funny. I've seen movies. I know what happens when you get put in an unmarked van."

"What happens?" he asked, faking distress.

She knew he was teasing her with his questions. Still, she couldn't help herself. Oddly, she felt comfortable around him.

"They fish your body out of a river after showing unflattering pictures of you all over the media in hopes someone has spotted you. In reality, you're already swimming with the fishes."

"And they told you they were going to kill you?" he asked, still looking amused. "Interesting."

"Like serial killers inform you of their intent." She huffed, waving a hand in the air frantically to get her point across. "They claimed they just wanted to talk. Pfft. Do I look stupid? No way was I going anywhere with them."

"So you evaded them three times," he mused.

"I did." She almost asked how he knew, but had a hunch he was with them. "I went to the police once for help."

"How did that work out for you?"

She bit the corner of her lip. "They held me in a cell, and when they opened it, a guy from one of the groups who tried to take me was there. He'd bailed me out. That is pretty twisted, don't you think?"

"Not if he was really trying to help you." Eadan shook his head. "And what did you do then?"

"Faked being sick. When they went for help, I ran. No way was I letting a group of nutjobs steal me away to take me apart in tiny pieces and dissect me."

He laughed. The entirely too sexy jerk actually laughed at her. "You mean a member of the group who has been trying to get you, bring you in safely, and tell you about the actual bad guys?"

She stilled. Wait. The men in black weren't the enemy? How could that be? She'd spent so long believing them to be the ultimate threat. Dare she believe Eadan? Jimmy would tell her to trust her gut in this situation. He'd say she had to follow her instincts. Her gut said Eadan was on the level. That he was being honest. And years of drawing him, sketching every detail of his face, left her feeling a bond to him. One she didn't want to see broken now that she knew he was actually a flesh-and-blood man, not just a figment of her imagination.

"Oh. So they aren't the bad guys?"

"No. Well, the majority of them aren't. It's complicated. Suffice to say, I'm not a bad guy." He began touching the walls of the container. He hissed and pulled his hand back. "Lead." She watched him as he jerked on his chains. "I'm betting these are lead laced as well."

Stories Jimmy used to tell her of other types of supernaturals came back to her. Her eyes widened. Excitement raced through her. "You're a faerie!"

He responded with a slight laugh. "I am."

"That is so cool," she said, sounding very child-like. She didn't care. She'd always wanted to meet a faerie. "Are you a Trooping Faerie?'

"Am I a what?"

She smiled wider. "Can you fly?"

He paused in his search for a way out. He faced her direction. "Do I look like a pixie to you?"

She eyed him. "Well, no, but I've never seen one, so maybe."

"They're smaller than me. Much smaller."

"And they can fly?"

The look he gave her made her blush. "No, they don't fly like in the normal sense of the word. They levitate and can suspend themselves in midair for a period of time. I guess it gives the illusion of flight." He huffed. "Why are we talking about them again?"

"I thought *you* were one."

He shot her a hard look. Oddly, it just turned her on. Under normal circumstances her temper would have gotten the better of her and she'd have added to someone's injuries. Not this someone. He was different.

She just wasn't sure how or why.

Flashes of how it felt to touch him washed over her. She had to put her thoughts on something else and fast. The next she knew she was blurting out, "How old are you? Are you, like, a thousand? A friend of mine told me he knew some faeries that were pushing a thousand."

Eadan exhaled slowly. It was evident he was trying to be patient with her. "I'm going to be thirty-one soon."

Some of her elation waned. "Great. I dreamed up the baby faerie."

"Baby faerie?" he questioned. "Do I look like a baby to you?"

Hell no. He looked like he'd be a killer in bed. Something about him oozed sexuality. Even beat up he gave off a vibe that said "once I take you, you'll never want another". She swallowed hard, remembering the feel of his chest. "Um, no. Not really so much."

"And for the record, we prefer the term Fae to faerie."

"Sounds more manly. I can see why," she said, before thinking better of it.

He snorted and then went all the way around the container, to no avail. She suspected his eyesight wasn't quite as good as her shifter one was, so she didn't bother pointing out that his mission had been a lost cause. They were locked in.

"So," she started, "what is it your organization wants with me, Eadan?"

He returned to her and sat again, looking tired and sore. "We're called PSI."

She merely listened as he continued on.

"We deal in paranormal security and intelligence. Intel came in on you," he said softly. "It led us to believe you might be a child of the Asia Project."

"Asia Project?" she asked. She'd heard Jimmy mention it once in passing to one of his contacts.

"Bad guys doing bad things to babies, hoping to make super soldiers, or the at least, the next wave of super humans."

She was quiet for a while as she let what he said soak in. "And you think I'm one of these babies from the Asia Project?"

"We know you are," he said. He watched her in a way that made her feel as though she was the sexiest woman put on the face of the Earth. Not the street rat she really was. "We were able to track down your adoption records."

She shook her head. "Not possible. My adoptive parents got me from a backwoods orphanage overseas. The place had a fire. All its records were destroyed."

Eadan touched her hand with his and heat shot through her. "PSI swept in during the fire, grabbing what they could and reconstructing as much evidence and information as possible. They took the copies and got rid of the rest. They needed to protect your identity and the identity of others like you who were funneled through the same orphanage."

There were others like her? Others who didn't know what they were or why they were this way? She turned her hand, taking Eadan's in hers. "Did you find them all? The others?"

He shook his head. "No. You're the first one from *this* orphanage we've been able to locate. And you're hard to pin down long enough to bring in and tell everything to."

She blushed. "In my defense, I thought you people wanted to dissect me or leave me in a river."

"No. We don't do that sort of thing." He held her hand and lifted it, his chains rattling. "We gave that up some time in the early twenties."

Sensing he was joking, her lips twitched before giving in and smiling. "You hear this from the old timers?"

"Oh yeah, they sit around talking about the good ole days." He met her gaze. "When you could just toss whoever you wanted in the river and be done with them."

"Glad I missed out on that," she said.

He stared at her for the longest time. "You're too thin."

She knew. *It's not like I can help it.*

"I never said it was your fault," he said, surprising her.

She tipped her head, watching him, wondering if he'd really read her mind.

"I'm going to get you out of here and then I'm going to feed you."

She grinned. "Sounds like a plan. But I did have a banana before you so rudely walked in on me getting cleaned up."

He flashed a wicked grin that screamed sex. What was with him? Every action he did in some way made her think naughty thoughts. "I'd say I was sorry but… And I saw your work with that apple. Impressive," he said.

She laughed and it felt good to do so after so long of finding little joy in anything. She understood their circumstances were not a laughing matter, but it beat crying her eyes out. That wouldn't fix anything. As soon as she thought about tears, she found some wanting to come. She looked away, hoping Eadan's eyesight wasn't good in the low light.

He held her hand tighter. "Inara?"

"Hmm?"

He caressed her hand with his thumb. "Tell me about your sketches."

She froze. He knew about them? How? "I don't want to talk about them."

Eadan kissed the back of her hand and warmth continued to spread throughout her. Now wasn't the time to develop wet panties for a guy she'd just met. Now was time to hold her shit together, figure a way out, and go to ground again. As Eadan planted another kiss on her hand, she got the feeling she wouldn't go anywhere without him.

She pulled on her courage and leaned her head against his shoulder. "I don't know why I draw you. I just do."

"How long have you been doing it?"

She shrugged. "I don't know. Since forever. What does it mean?"

He said nothing.

She groaned. "I sold a few. Naked ones."

"There are naked drawings of me out in the world?" he asked.

She shrugged and was about to comment but decided against it. Didn't seem important now considering the mess they were in.

He put his head to hers and they sat in silence for a while. She was upset he didn't answer the question, but got the sense she might not like what he had to say if he did, so she left it alone. Besides, it felt good to be near him. She ran her other hand over his shackle. "The lead, it stops you from being able to use your magik?"

"Yes."

"And it burns you, doesn't it?" she asked, seeing his skin now looked raw where the shackles touched.

"I'm fine."

Guilt assailed her. She opened her mouth and words came flooding out, "When you were out cold, I was petting your chest. I'm sorry. I couldn't help myself. *You* try not touching you."

SIX

IT TOOK all of Eadan's control to avoid laughing at Inara's obviously sincere apology. She'd touched him that way? He was pissed he'd missed it. The very idea of her hands on his body made his cock stir to life again. Eadan had to fight to keep from kissing the back of her hand. It was enough she was permitting him to touch her. He didn't want to push too far.

He should stop and look for another way out, yet he couldn't seem to pull himself from her side. For the moment, he was where he needed to be.

"Are you mad?" she asked. The vulnerability in her voice moved him. "That makes me one of those creepy people, doesn't it?"

"Tell you what," he answered, looking for

words to set her mind at ease. "Let's get out of here and you can pet me as much as you want, okay?"

"Promise?" She blinked. "I mean, um, I'm good. It's all good."

Hell yeah, it was fine with him if she petted him. She could rub him all over. He'd welcome it. But as much as he wanted to remain in contact with her, they needed out of the container and fast. Helmuth knew enough to put him in lead-laced chains and a lead-lined box. That meant he fully understood who and what Eadan was—that he was Fae.

And that meant PSI had a mole. Helmuth's men shouldn't have been expecting him. Yet, clearly they were.

Dammit.

Inara tugged on his hand, returning his full attention to her.

"When you were out cold, and I was petting you, it suddenly felt and sounded like hundreds of bees were buzzing around us." She turned her face away from him. "And your head healed when it happened."

Eadan gasped. Her Fae side had responded

to his, as a mate would. She'd healed him without realizing what she'd done.

She is my true mate.

"I'm your true what?" she asked.

Eadan grinned. She could read his thoughts. As a mate should be able to. Though, she didn't seem to have registered she had. He'd seen this happen to couples before. Sometimes, they tried to rationalize what was happening before admitting to the strange and wonderful.

Grabbing her and holding her close before claiming her as a Fae male would was all he wanted to do. Their current predicament demanded he postpone that desire, however difficult that may be. It was especially hard because Eadan's line of Fae derived power from sex. It intensified their gifts.

She looked at him and tried to pull her hand free from his. "I'm sorry. I don't know why it happened or even really understand what happened."

He kept hold of her hand, bringing it to his lips once again. He kissed it and noticed she closed her eyes, leaning in to him more. That was a good thing. It meant they trusted one another on a baser level. It was elemental, as it should be. "Inara, you healed me. Like a mate would."

"A mate?" she asked.

"We can talk about that later."

A confused expression covered her face. "How could I heal you? I'm not magik."

"You're more magik than you realize," he responded.

Skepticism entered her green gaze. "No. I just touched you and then…then there was a buzzing. It increased when—" She looked to the floor, seeming entirely too interested in it. "Never mind."

He fought the urge to grin. She was sexually shy and he found that endearing as all get out. Since his line of Fae were sexual by nature, it was refreshing to have a woman like Inara near him. There was an innocence about her that made him question Jack's statement that she might be romantically linked with James Hagen.

His temper began to rise but he held firm, refusing to allow it to ruin the small exchanges between them. "The buzz grew when you were aroused, correct?" he asked, already knowing the answer to his question.

She groaned. "Yes. Fine. It did. What does that mean?"

"That we can heal one another through sexual energy."

She jerked her hand free from his and stood. He made no move to go after her. She needed to feel safe with him. He understood that. He'd read what little had been in her file. She'd had a rough go of it. Life hadn't been kind and he was guessing he'd probably never get all the gritty details out of her. He'd give her all the time he could, considering their situation, to come to terms with everything. He sat still, watching her move, memorizing the sway of her hips, silently wanting them swaying above him as she rode him.

She twisted and looked at his wrists. "The lead, it hurts you, right?"

"I said I was fine." Eadan didn't want her concerned with him.

"You lied," she corrected. "You're not fine."

She had him there. He nodded.

Inara approached him slowly, as if she were prey nearing a predator. Her actions were cautious. He remained in place, knowing it helped her feel in control of the situation. She moved to her knees and reached out a tentative hand to him. Her fingers skimmed his wrists and her bottom lip began to tremble. As moisture coated her green eyes, his chest tightened. The struggle within her was evident. She wanted to help him but was scared of what helping him might mean. It was too much for anyone, especially someone her age. He couldn't blame her.

"Inara, I'm fine. I'll heal this on my own at some point. I don't want you to do anything you don't want to do." He meant every word he said. He'd rather have his hands fall clean off than cause her a moment of emotional or physical pain.

Because she's your mate and that is what mates do for one another.

"I could heal you though, right?"

He pressed his lips together a moment. "I don't want you doing anything you don't want to—"

She launched herself at him, knocking him backward. He fell with her in his arms. He absorbed the impact of their bodies hitting the floor. The feel of her body pressed to his caused him to gasp, opening his mouth to hers. Her lips met his and Eadan's eyes widened as she thrust her tongue into his mouth. He gave up trying to reason with her and simply gave in to her kiss.

She purred and the sound drove his lust into overdrive. Power began to build around them. It shouldn't have been able to, with the lead chains and lead-lined container, yet it was.

True mates.

The power latched on to Eadan's and blended with it, intensifying everything on his body, making him feel her even more. Her hands were everywhere at once, tugging at his shirt before pushing it up his torso as best she could. The fucking chains restricted both their movements.

Their tongues intertwined, driving the sex lust onward. Grinding himself up against her mound more, he could sense her nearing culmination. Damn, his woman was fiery and responded to touch beautifully.

Magik continued to beat at the air around them. Had Eadan been free from the chains, he knew his power would have removed their clothing already. It could do that and so much more.

Inara pushed down on him, her jaw going slack. "Ohmygod!"

He knew then she was coming. The power around them grew to epic proportions. Eadan tried to control it in some fashion but couldn't. The next he knew it felt as if tiny strings were threading between them. Try as he might to stop it, he was powerless in the face of the sex magik. They were true mates and they were doing what true mates did when they shared power—they were forever cementing the bond between them. Should he actually slip his cock into her and share his seed with her, they would be husband and wife in the eyes of the supernatural community. It would be an unbreakable bond. Already they'd laid the groundwork for it. Already they would forever be tied to one another.

Slow down. She needs a say in this.

Eadan's pulse raced with each caress of her hands over his torso. Her kisses came faster, more desperate than before. He knew then the power building was affecting her as well. The faerie in them both craved this, craved sex and stimulation.

Growling, he flipped her onto her back gently, his body moving over hers. He had to have more of her and fast. Taking the lead with the kiss, he circled her tongue, drawing tiny moans of passion from her. His cock, ready for sex, was painfully hard. Inara wrapped her legs around his waist, biting at his lower lip and moaning a moan that screamed sex. Her sweet taste and eager kisses spurred him onward as he ground against her mound. Each swipe, each rotation of his hips, elicited gasps from her. As she dug her fingers into his upper arms, she pressed her mouth to his ear.

"Please."

His lips found hers once more and he smiled against them. It was good she wanted him too. Good that the gods had selected right for them. Eadan wanted to stroke her face and feel his way down her, undressing her slowly, but the chains prevented that.

Dammit.

There was too much clothing between them. He needed in her and soon or he'd burst like a teenage boy. She pushed against him, her movements as hungry as he felt. If she kept rubbing on him like that, he'd come in his jeans and embarrass himself.

She grabbed his backside and squeezed. "I need you."

He needed her too. She'd already begun to fill the void he had in his heart. The hollow pit he thought would remain empty and fester with angst and bitterness. In the short time he'd known Inara she'd already began to chase away the loneliness, push back the darkness and heal the damage that had been done to his heart so long ago.

Her tongue danced around his. Fuck, the woman could kiss.

The power continued to build. She'd been close in her saying it felt like bees buzzing around them. It did. Energy and strength poured into him. He knew it was doing the same to her. She needed it. She'd been so drained when he'd first met her.

His system jolted as she put her fingers down the top of his jeans. Raw need bore through him but it brought with it something else—the knowledge this was too much, too soon. He was about to take his mate on the floor of a container.

Like an animal.

He stopped everything and pulled off her, careful with the chains as one caught in her hair. He worked it out gently and eased back, shaking his head. Eadan took large deep breaths. "Inara, no. We can't. Not like this. Not here."

"Oh, we can," she protested, and made a move to tackle him again. He had to hand it to her, she was motivated, for sure. She grabbed the top of his jeans, her fingers skimming his skin and making him second guess the higher road he was attempting to take.

He wanted to slide into her, to take what she was offering, but he couldn't. Not under these circumstances. More importantly, not without her knowing the truth. That if they did, she'd be his wife. He nearly kicked himself for having morals as he said, "No."

She paused in her mission to get his jeans fully undone. Confusion knitted her brow. "You don't want me?"

"I fucking want you so bad I can't even begin to put it into words, but this isn't how I want you. I want to take you when we're not locked up. When it's safe. When I can spend hours upon hours pleasing you."

Her cheeks flamed red. She drew back from him slightly. "Hours and hours? People have sex that long?"

He watched her and a sinking feeling came over him. "Inara, have you had sex before?"

She shook her head and refused to look at him. "No."

Fuck. He'd nearly taken her virginity on a dirty container floor. Eadan touched her chin, forcing her to meet his gaze. "I'm sorry. I shouldn't have let it go this far. I couldn't help myself."

She snorted. "You couldn't help yourself? I've wanted to jump your bones since you walked in on me getting washed up. Trust me when I say between the two of us, it's me with the control issues here."

His cock begged to differ. He held his tongue on the matter.

She touched his wrists. "It worked. They're healed. Still bound, but at least they aren't raw anymore."

"How do you feel?"

"Horny," she responded with a silly grin. "Actually, I feel the best I've felt in years. Why?"

He caressed her cheek again, his finger easing over her lip. "It goes both ways."

She blinked up at him. "Why do I feel this

way with you? Trust me when I say this isn't something I've done with anyone else."

He bent and kissed her chastely, wanting more but holding back. He put his forehead to hers. "You drew pictures of me before you even met me."

She nodded, keeping her head to his. "Why? The mate thing?"

He snickered softly. "Yes. The mate thing."

"What, exactly, does it mean? Is it a husband and wife thing?"

"Think bigger."

She gasped.

He kissed her again.

There was movement near the far end of the container and then the sounds of something scratching near the door. Eadan pushed to his feet, pulled Inara up and forced her behind him just as the door opened.

Light spilled in and it took his eyes a second to adjust to it. A tall redhead stood there, concern in her eyes. "Are you two okay?"

Inara pushed out from behind Eadan. "Jinx?"

"Thank the gods!" the woman shouted. "I've been looking for you for two days!"

"We've been locked up for two days?" Inara asked.

The woman nodded and waved her hand toward them. "Hurry up. Helmuth's men are being distracted by my girls. They won't be gone long. You need to get the hell out of here. He's got bad plans for you," she said to Inara.

Eadan caught Inara's arm. "Hold on. Who is this?"

"We can trust her," Inara said, and he believed her. She took his chained hand in hers. "Let's go, Eadan."

SEVEN

JON LOOKED through his sniper scope, trained on the door of the warehouse. When the thirty-six-hour mark passed without any word or check-in from Eadan about his mission or how he was doing on it, Jon had started to worry. He decided to say screw the higher-ups and he ignored Colonel Brooks's order to leave Eadan be on this mission. It had taken some doing, but Jon was able to track down Eadan. Thankfully, Roi was able to get Missy to give her father big sad eyes while she worked up some fake tears. General Newman caved. Spilled all the details. Didn't matter.

He was going to be pissed, but Jon didn't care. He wouldn't lose another brother.

He'd not been the only I-Op to think so.

They'd all come with him, wanting to help Eadan. Even Roi seemed anxious to make sure "blondie" wasn't harmed.

Damn good thing he'd basically said "fuck you" to his orders, because from what Jon had been able to piece together since his arrival on the scene, Eadan was in deep shit. No one had seen or heard from him in forty-eight hours.

A number of lowlifes were willing to talk for motivation of the green kind. After paying off some thugs, Jon was able to find out that Eadan was still on the premises. Though he couldn't get a direct bead on him. The wards up around the area were interfering with his ability to hear and smell. His shifter traits were useless. Thankfully he'd been a solider long before he'd been a shifter.

He returned to surveying the scene through his scope.

The same group of men had moved from a ship docked just off the pier near the warehouse. They'd followed a group of scantily dressed women back into the warehouse.

A redheaded woman had then boarded the ship. The whole thing smacked of trouble and

Eadan was no doubt in the center of it. That damn Fae could get himself into some jams.

He gets us out of a lot too.

The men spoke amongst themselves a moment before one looked in the direction of the ship. He pointed and the others all took off running in that direction. Jon set his sights on the ship and was surprised to see the redheaded woman there, opening a cargo container.

INARA nearly cried tears of joy as she hurried towards Jinx. Confused for a moment as to what she was seeing behind Jinx, Inara came a stop just shy of the end of the container. Why was she looking at water? "What in the world?"

"We're in a cargo container that has apparently been loaded on a freighter," Eadan responded, still close to her, his hand in hers. "They had plans to move us. My guess is, they'd take us to foreign soil. They'd have a better shot at keeping us hidden there."

Eadan removed his hand from hers and stepped behind her, lifting her and setting her on the ground gently. He hopped down and put his body between Jinx and Inara once more. He remained close to her, his hand on her low back.

"We can trust her." Touching his arm, Inara smiled.

He raised a brow and looked Jinx over carefully. "She's nymph and succubus."

Inara shrugged. Whatever Jinx was, she was on the level. "We can trust her. She is friends with someone I trust."

Eadan stiffened. "James Hagen?"

James?

Gasping, Jinx snatched hold of Eadan's hand, and for a moment all Inara saw was green. She didn't want any woman touching her man.

My man?

She gulped and calmed. Shouting for everyone to hear that she had staked a claim on Eadan seemed unwise. Plus, she hadn't exactly talked to him about her stake of ownership.

"Do you know where Jimmy is?" Jinx asked, staring Eadan in the eyes. There was a note of desperation that moved Inara.

He'd dead. He has to be. He wouldn't leave me on my own this long if he wasn't.

She felt it in her bones. Inara waited for

Eadan's answer as to where Jimmy was, if he was even alive. She'd spent a long time learning from Jimmy, and he'd never once mentioned anyone named Eadan.

Eadan's entire body remained tense. "Last I saw him was when he was standing beside a fallen agent. He'd gotten the man killed and then he turned his back on all of us."

Jinx laughed partially under her breath. "You're young, Fae. What you think you know and what is true are two very different things."

Inara got the sense Eadan was about to lose his shit. She caressed his inner arm, his muscles making need race through her. Jinx's eyes swirled with a multitude of colors and she grinned, looking so erotic it was nearly scary. "Mmm, sex energy. You've bonded."

"Bonded?" questioned Inara.

"We need to get the hell out of here." Eadan ignored the question.

"Agreed." Jinx motioned to Inara. "My girls have the guards occupied. They won't be able to distract them for long."

"Your girls?" Eadan glanced from Inara to Jinx.

Jinx swayed her hips. "I run a brothel for

supernaturals. My girls are paid very well and they love their jobs. So no lectures. Okay? Besides, I get the sense you understand exactly the types of supernaturals who can't live without sex."

Eadan looked to the warehouse along the pier they were docked at. Men emerged from the side door, their sights on Eadan and Inara. Eadan took her by the shoulders and bent, his lips capturing hers, his kiss making her knees weak. When he drew back, she went to her tiptoes, trying to get more.

"Go with your friend."

He wanted her to go without him? Why? They'd been through so much and she'd dreamed of him long before all of this. He couldn't possibly want to separate now. Not after what they'd shared. "Jinx said there is a way out. We can both go," she protested.

"Go!" he shouted, causing her to jump.

She shook her head and Jinx grabbed her, yanking on her with strength that actually surprised Inara. "No. I won't leave him."

"They want you," Jinx said. "Not him. He knows this. They planned to test some theories. At least that is what I overheard Helmuth saying to his right-hand man. Then they were going to kill the Fae. Inara, what they plan for you… It's not… We need to go."

Inara didn't know who they were or what they wanted with her. She just knew she wouldn't leave Eadan. "No!"

"Go!" Eadan shouted again.

Hurt that he'd want her away from him, she stopped struggling. "Eadan?"

Averting his gaze, he spoke in a low tone. "We shared a moment while captured. Nothing more."

She nearly took offense, but realized what he was doing—protecting her. Trying to get her to go. "Bullshit."

He blinked at her with wide eyes.

"You're lying again," she protested, jerking free from Jinx's grasp. "We shared something a hell of a lot more. Admit it."

He looked pained. "Dammit, woman, go. I'll hold them off. Jinx will get you to safety."

"What about you?"

Jinx tugged on her. "Don't make me use my magik. I will to protect you. Jimmy would have wanted it. He loved you like a daughter."

Something in Eadan's expression changed. He nodded. "Go. Please. I'll be fine. I promise."

She didn't believe him.

Jinx put her mouth to Inara's ear. "If you stay, there is a hundred percent chance he will get himself killed attempting to protect you. You're his mate. It's easy enough to tell by the bond you've shared. He won't fight with a clear head if you're near him."

Inara didn't want to go, but she understood the truth behind Jinx's words. She swallowed hard and then launched herself at Eadan, kissing him with all her being. The buzzing returned and she willed all the energy she could into him. She jerked back. "Come back to me."

He looked horny as hell. "Oh, you can bank on that, beautiful."

Eadan ran down the ramp and made a left, right for the men headed in their direction. Jinx led Inara down the ramp but dragged her right. Inara didn't want to leave Eadan to fend for himself.

Suddenly, people seemed to be coming in from all angles. It took her a second to realize the spectators were coming to view the pending fight.

Sick bastards.

A huge guy with onyx eyes and dark brown hair that hung to nearly his shoulders pushed past her, touching her shoulder. "I'll help him," he said, his voice deep.

Jinx smiled wide. "Duke, you got my call!"

"Thanks for the heads-up. I was given bad intel," he said. "I got this, Red. Get the girl to safety." He pushed his way through the people gathering around Eadan. One of the men tried to attack Duke. He twisted, his hand shifting forms as he took the man out at the throat with one blow.

Inara sucked in a big breath.

"Duke will help Eadan," Jinx said. "We need to get out of here."

"Who are you, really?" She stared at the woman. She was far more than the fancy madam she presented herself to be.

Jinx shrugged. "Someone who knows how to the play the game and who knows when it's time to call in reinforcements."

EIGHT

EADAN TURNED IN A CIRCLE, watching as the enemy moved in around him. He'd keep Helmuth's men back while Inara got to safety. He didn't care what he had to do. The only thing he knew beyond a shadow of a doubt was that she was not to be harmed in any way.

My mate above my life.

People spilled out of the warehouse. More and more came, and Eadan suspected they sensed a fight about to happen and didn't want to miss it since they'd paid to view the nightly death matches.

Helmuth's men tried to separate, to divide and conquer. Eadan couldn't let them get to Inara. Urgency and the fierce need to protect her at all costs consumed him. Hot, raw power raced through him, defying the chains and what they stood for. His magik continued to increase at a rate he'd never felt it do before. The sex magik they'd conjured within the container helped greatly to rebuild his strength. The thought of Inara being in Helmuth's clutches tipped him over the edge of sanity.

Narrowing his gaze on the enemy, he smiled a smile that promised no mercy. A second later his magik shot through him, making his body bend forward and then snap upright, breaking away his shackles. The chains fell to the ground, clanking loudly. The men hesitated but came at him all the same.

Morons.

Eadan spun around and kicked one so hard he went airborne. As he turned back, ready to strike, he stopped just shy of punching Duke Marlow in the face. "Duke?"

Grinning, the werewolf pursed his lips in a kissing motion. "Miss me?"

"You're late," Eadan said sternly. He'd given up hope Duke would arrive at all. Part of him had begun to worry Duke had been killed, or worse yet, decided to switch sides. Eadan should have known better. Duke was as loyal as they came and wouldn't miss a fight regardless what shape he was in.

Upright or full of bullet holes.

That was just Duke.

"Hey, blame the person who relayed my orders. They sent me bad intel," Duke said, turning and taking out an enemy as he ranted. "I ended up in the middle of a cartel deal going way wrong. Fucking spent two days dodging them and trying to get back to the airstrip before I said to hell with it and attacked full force. Imagine their surprise when I shifted into a wolf and nearly ate one."

Eadan groaned.

Duke continued, "I had to catch another fuckin' flight and hurry my ass here. I hate to fly. I hate eating cartel members more. They have a tendency to come back up on you later. Fuckers give me indigestion."

Eadan ducked, allowing the newest attacker to go up and over his back. When the man landed and came at him, Eadan thrust magik into him. In an instant, the man burst into a ball of flames.

Duke's dark eyes widened. "They pissed you off good, huh?"

"They touched my woman," Eadan said evenly, though he wanted to explode and light the entire fucking area on fire. He managed to restrain himself.

"Whatcha talkin' 'bout? When did you get a woman?" Duke asked, kicking the shit out of another of Helmuth's men. He barely paid any mind to the men as he spoke. "This a mate thing?"

"It is."

He whistled through his teeth. "Sucks to be these guys."

Eadan throat punched another man, and once he was down, he grabbed him by the top of his hair. "Where is Helmuth?"

"G-gone," the man stammered as best he could, holding Eadan's wrist. "We were to take you to him at a new location. You and the bitch."

Eadan twisted the man's head fast, snapping his neck. His breathing was harsh and heavy. "My woman is not a bitch!"

"You ran off to be one of those I-Ops," Duke said harshly. "They left you to fend for yourself, huh?"

No sooner did the words come out of his

mouth than the next enemy trying to come at them dropped, a crimson dot appearing on his forehead, right between his eyes.

Jon.

Eadan laughed. "Nah, they were just late to the party too."

"That their doing?" asked Duke, tossing away a puny shifter.

Eadan thrust magik at more of Helmuth's men, wondering how many the seedy asshole had. Apparently, a lot. "Yep."

"Nice."

Jon took out two more. There was a flash of black and suddenly Lukian and Roi were next to him. Lukian looked to Duke and nodded. "Duke."

Duke's forehead crinkled. "Wait, Lukian, you're one of the I-Ops?"

"I am."

Roi laughed. "Sucks finding out the guy you call king lowers himself to manual labor, huh?" Roi dove at two shifters and tackled them to the ground.

He was having way too much fun with this.

Wilson and Green rushed in next. Green held a limp vampire by the neck.

"This one spilled everything," he said, dropping the vampire. "Molyneux has a den of vampires near here. They're in league with Helmuth."

"They appear to be one vampire short," Lukian said.

Wilson drew his lips back. "Actually, they're about a den short. Sorry, Green and I got held up killing already-dead guys."

The bodies were piled up around the area. The remaining bad guys shared a look and took off running in all directions. They looked like scattering rats. Eadan would have said as much out loud, but Wilson took enough shit for being a wererat. He didn't need any more.

"Wait!" he heard Jinx yell.

Eadan spun around to find Inara running right at him. She ran right past two of Helmuth's men Eadan had assumed were fleeing.

They're going for Inara, he thought.

No, beautiful, he pushed with his mind. *Run the other way!*

Inara faltered in her step and stumbled forward. Before Eadan could so much as blink, one of the men had hold of her and was ripping her off the ground. Eadan's magik went wild and nearly burst free of him. He had to fight to control it as he ran in her direction. He could harm her by mistake if he wasn't careful.

Inara stunned him as she came up fast, ramming her hand into the nose of her attacker. She rolled over the man's back and kicked out with both feet at the other, hitting him in the chest and sending him flying backward. She landed on her feet, crouched and stared up at the man who had blood gushing from his nose. She looked like a predator.

A woman ready to kill if need be.

He couldn't have been a prouder mate if he tried. Though, he'd rather she never have to lift a finger to defend herself again.

He made it to her and killed the men quickly before pulling her into his embrace. Jinx appeared next to him, looking winded. "I tried to stop her."

"I know. Thank you," he said. He held his woman to him, happy she was alive. He kissed the top of her head. "I'm fine, beautiful. You should have stayed with Jinx."

Inara sobbed openly. "I was afraid for you."
"Shh."

Suddenly, Eadan was ripped back from her. He prepared to attack the person with magik but stopped when he realized it was Roi.

Roi looked livid. "Keep your goddamn hands off her!"

"W-what?" Eadan asked.

Lukian came to a stop next to Roi and Eadan waited for the captain to rein in Roi as he always did. Instead, Lukian's posture went rigid. "Step away from the girl."

Duke strolled past them both without a care in the world. Typical Duke. "I say take her home and fuck her."

"I agree with that one," Inara said, stunning Eadan.

"Absolutely not!" shouted Lukian.

Eadan stared at them and Jack's words came back to him. *They'll see her as a sister.* Sighing, Eadan loosened his hold on Inara, knowing if he didn't, things would only go from bad to worse. He held her hand instead. "Beautiful, we'll get you to safety."

Duke stopped next to Jinx. "Want to grab a drink?"

"I want to grab a bottle," she said.

"What about Helmuth?" asked Eadan. "He has to know you double-crossed him."

She shrugged. "I have friends in high places. He should be scared of me."

Duke laughed and put his arm out to escort Jinx from the scene full of dead bodies.

Eadan looked around. "We made a huge mess."

"A cleanup team will handle it," Green said. "We should get a move on."

NINE

INARA WASN'T sure what a secret government facility would look like, but this wasn't what she had in mind. Too many movies and too much TV while growing up had given her a false sense of what she might find. She thought armed guards, all looking cookie-cutter, would be lining the area. She assumed there would be a checkpoint with several of those same guards, demanding to see their credentials.

Something.

Nope.

Nothing.

They'll let anyone in.

Eadan laughed softly, squeezing her hand more. "No, beautiful, it's secure."

"Hmm?" she asked before thinking better of it. He'd done it again. He'd guessed her thoughts. Whatever kind of Fae he was, it was powerful. Was he why she'd heard his voice in her head before?

They drove up to an automatic fence that didn't really look that imposing. Green rolled down his window, keyed in a number and then put his thumb to a pad. It had to be a good sign if that sort of technology was involved, right? The fence slid open, allowing them to pass through. The SUV behind them followed close.

She wondered if they ever got the hot-tempered guy named Roi calmed down. Probably not. Seemed like he had some anger issues.

They all sort of did.

"What is it you all do?" she asked.

They all looked to man in the passenger seat. He was in charge. She'd gathered that much on the pier and then in the jet on the way there. He cast a warm smile in her direction that faltered when he spotted her hand in Eadan's. "We do things others can't. We don't exist, therefore, we don't follow the same rules. And we deal with things humans couldn't possibly understand."

"Captain is right," Green said. "Think of us as ghost soldiers, almost."

"Okay, if you want to freak me the hell out," she mumbled, partially under her breath.

Eadan and the others laughed. He kissed her temple. "They're all safe. I promise."

"I know, but still. This is all kind of a lot to process." She leaned into him.

The captain guy growled and she knew a warning when she heard one. She had half a mind to slap him on the head. She stared wide-eyed at him. "Would you please stop? It's uncalled for."

She wasn't sure why she said it.

Green stiffened and then his shoulders moved up and down. He was laughing at her.

Jerk.

"Lukian," Eadan said. "You and Roi have been acting strange."

That was putting it mildly. Lukian had piloted. Roi had to be taken to a back room by Wilson while Green and the one with amber eyes were left to babysit her and Eadan. These men were so weird.

Lukian grumbled and then faced forward. "I don't know. I just don't like you holding her hand. I don't think any man should be touching her."

Green laughed so hard, Inara wondered how he could see where he was driving. Whatever he found funny was lost on her. They sat in tension-filled silence as Green pulled the SUV into an underground parking garage. They exited and Eadan stayed close to her, his hand in hers. She didn't want to let go of him. She was damn happy he seemed to be suffering from the same problem she was.

The elevator was large. Biggest one she'd ever seen. The other men from the SUV that had followed them from the airport joined them. The hot-tempered one snarled, showing fangs when he spotted Eadan holding her hand.

Inara leapt in front of Eadan and stunned herself by stomping on the snarling guy's foot. He yelped and backed away.

Eadan tried to lift her but she elbowed him, holding her ground. She pointed at the snarly man. "Knock it off."

He pursed his lips. "I will if he stops touching you."

"You're not my boss."

"Children," Green said, still laughing. "Let's get upstairs and get this all sorted out with Colonel Brooks. I'm guessing he's not pleased with us at the moment."

Wilson eased up alongside her. "I'm fine with you and Eadan touching. I think it's great he found his mate."

"If you say so," mumbled the amber-eyed man as he went to the back corner and put an unlit cigarette in his mouth.

She looked up at Eadan. "He's got a lot of angst."

"You get used to it." Eadan bent and kissed her chastely on the lips.

Hot-temper snarled again.

"Roi," Green said, motioning to the elevator control panel. "Would you do the honors?"

Hot-tempered Roi pushed the button for level one.

Inara stuck her tongue out at him when they exited. He did a double take and then shook his head. He nudged Lukian. "You tell her she can't be with him."

Wilson put his hands up. "Whoa! You're acting like she's family or something. Calm down. She's a grown woman. She can do who and what she wants."

Jon had to push into the mix to protect Wilson as both Lukian and Roi went at him. A gentleman with black hair but salt and pepper temples stepped out of a room and into the hall. He lifted a brow at the scene. "Lukian?"

"Colonel Brooks, tell Inara she can't be near Eadan," Lukian said, sounding very young.

Brooks surveyed the men and then focused on Green. Wise man. Seemed the most level-headed choice. "Care to enlighten me?"

"I read the test results PSI had on Inara on the flight home. Let me get her checked over first, sir, and then I'll brief everyone."

"In the meantime, Eadan and the rest of you, come with me." The man motioned to them all.

"I go where Inara goes," said Eadan.

"No. She is going for a checkup and you're coming with me. General Newman is on the way." Brooks crossed his arms over his chest.

Inara allowed Green to lead her down the long corridor. It was high-end with fancy lighting and paintings on the walls that she knew cost big money. She loved art and spent time in so many art museums that she'd lost count. Art museums didn't charge to enter, and since she had no money, it worked out great.

Eadan remained behind, nodding as she glanced back at him. He made a move to come with her, but the one they'd referred to as Colonel stopped him, shaking his head. The other men remaining behind converged on him, keeping him held there. Eadan didn't look too pleased, but he remained in place all the same.

"What are they doing to him?" she asked.

"He doesn't want to leave you. I can read it all over his face but I'm guessing he's having a hard time processing everything that has gone on. And I think he wants to give you time. That would be a very Eadan thing to do." Green touched her shoulder gently. "It will be fine. I promise. I just need to get you all checked over. While I'm doing that, Eadan and the others will be debriefed."

She watched him carefully, wondering what his deal was. She couldn't smell anything about any of the I-Ops team. They had no discerning scents. It was strange. Only Eadan did. Thinking of his scent, the way she smelled nature around him with the smell of man, made her pulse speed and her heart race. She felt her cheeks flush. In an effort to avoid making a fool of herself in front of Green, she decided to go with a joke. "What are you? Some sort of doctor for the weird and wacky?"

He smiled and she felt more at ease. "Yes. That is exactly what I am. Right this way."

She followed him into a large room that looked part of a state-of-the-art medical facility. Her jaw dropped. "You know how to work all this stuff?"

"I do. So does my mate," he said as he handed her a gown from a shelf. He pointed to another door. "You can change in there."

"You're mated?" asked Inara, needing to know more about mates.

"I am."

She held the gown close to her chest. Curiosity got the better of her. "What does it mean?"

Green took a seat on a stool, putting him closer to her level. "What does *mate* mean?"

She nodded.

He looked at her with compassion and scientific interest. Yeah, he'd picked the right profession. "Did Eadan tell you anything about mates?"

"He said they were two halves of a whole," she answered. "Or something along those lines."

Green chuckled as if he'd heard a very funny joke. Maybe he just thought the stripped-down explanation she received was amusing. "That would be correct. It would seem that each supernatural is gifted one perfect match. One person who fits them and them alone. With them a bond is formed and the unions can often produce children where children are normally difficult for paranormals."

She tugged at her lower lip, her mind full of endless questions for the man. "Eadan says we're mates. How do you know if someone is or isn't your mate."

"It's inborn. Your gut tells you that without them you couldn't go on."

Thinking back, she remembered how she'd felt on the pier when she'd had to leave Eadan. She also remembered the buzzing bees between them. "Do you feel energy of sorts?"

"I believe two people with enough magik or Fae in them would, yes." Green folded his hands before him on his lap, as if prepared to answer any questions she had for hours if need be.

It was hard not to like him.

"He claims I've got magik in me. I can't. I sneeze when I'm around a full-blood," she blurted.

Green's lips drew back. He remained pleasant as he spoke, "I'll do some more testing, but the information I was able to obtain via PSI already tells me quite a bit. I believe you're not allergic to magiks so much as your body craves it and suppressing that side of you causes this reaction to others of full-magik descent."

She mulled over his words, letting them soak in. "You're saying I have magik in me, and because I don't use it, I sneeze around people who do?"

"In a nutshell," he replied.

"Can you read each other's thoughts?"

Green nodded.

Well, that explained that then. She wasn't crazy. Eadan could hear what she was thinking and she could hear him.

She had one more question. "Is it strange to love your mate when you only really just met them?"

Green stood slowly. "Not at all."

Good, because I think I do love him.

He watched her. "Inara, you should know that between mates, there is a very high chance you will conceive a child regardless the precautions you take."

She gulped. She wasn't ready for children just yet.

Green smiled. "When it happens, it happens."

She held up the gown and walked past him to the door he'd pointed at. "I'll change."

The exam was quick and painless.

Green patted her shoulder. "All clear. I can give you some fluids. That might be best, just to be on the safe side."

"I'm fine. Eadan has promised me much in the way of food and drink," she joked.

"See to it you eat or I will not hesitate to haul your backside in here. Got it?"

She didn't doubt he would. She nodded. "Got it."

Inara drew back as Lukian and Roi burst through the door to the clinic area.

"What is taking so long?" Lukian asked, his voice hard.

Green barely seemed fazed by the two. He looked up from his computer screen and sighed. "I wondered how long it would be before you both showed up. I thought Eadan would beat you to it."

The men shared a look that screamed guilty.

Inara gasped. "What did you do to him?"

Roi whistled and looked upward. "No idea what you're talking about."

Green swiveled in his chair. "Roi, did you do something to Eadan?"

Roi pointed to Inara. "He wanted to touch her. She's too young to be touched. She's just a baby."

"She's twenty-three," corrected Green. He'd saved her the trouble of needing to point it out to them.

She had no idea why they kept behaving so strangely around her. They acted as if they were her father or something. She put her hands on her hips, annoyance making her take leave of her better judgment. "What the hell did you do to my man?"

Roi looked at Lukian. "She called him her man. We should kill him."

"What?" she demanded.

Lukian nodded. "I think you might be right."

Green shot out of his seat and went at them both, pushing them into the room and away from the door. "No one is killing anyone. Take a seat."

They glared at him.

Lukian puffed out his chest. "Move. That is an order."

"Sir, with respect, shut up and sit down," Green said, not budging an inch. He was hardly a small guy. Not that Lukian or Roi were either, but Inara had no doubts who was going to win if it came down to it.

Green.

The geeky science guy wasn't to be messed with.

He took a long, deep breath. "Sit."

They each took a seat on some of the stools in the room.

Green motioned with his hand at them. "Your behavior makes sense to me now that I've been able to go over all the data PSI had on Inara."

She was all ears.

"She's carrying your line of lycan." Green

stared hard at Lukian. "Your exact line. And from all accounts, she was born with it."

Lukian twisted and stared at Inara with wide eyes. He stood slowly, coming toward her. The closer he got, the more she considered backing away, but instead held her ground. He touched her cheek tenderly, in a loving manner, like her adoptive parents had long ago. His blue eyes moistened. "How did I not see it? You look just like her."

"Like who?"

"My sister, Imogen."

Roi came and stood next to Lukian. "You told me about her. You said she died during the lycan roundups over a hundred years ago."

"She did," Lukian said. "But her son didn't. I placed him with another family. Far from it all. Somewhere he'd be safe."

Roi shook his head. "Wait, you're saying Inara is a direct descendent from your line?"

"Yes," Green answered for Lukian. He walked closer, his shoulders slumping. "Sir, there is no listing for birth parents for Inara. Unlike the others we've found. From the notes I've been piecing together, I think her parents were killed and she was taken from them as an infant. The tests on her were done after she was born."

Lukian continued to touch her cheek.

"She has a good deal of Fae in her that was natural to her as well," Green added.

Lukian laughed. "I placed Imogen's son with the Fae. Culann of the Council of Fae Elders helped me to hide him. That is how we know one another so well." He pulled Inara into a big hug and held her so tight she half thought she'd break in two. "He took my nephew and put him somewhere even I couldn't find him. And he's never spoken of him again. I got the sense it was because something horrible happened to him."

She patted his back. "Nice werewolf. Can you let go of me now?"

Roi laughed and pulled her out of Lukian's embrace. "My turn to hug her."

He did and she simply stood in place. As she thought about it all, she gasped. "Wait. I'm your niece, sort of?"

Lukian smiled. "Yes, but within our kind, when the male father figure is no longer present, the next males in the line automatically take on the roles of brothers or father figures."

She looked between the two of them. "I'm

guessing you're both older than you look, but can we not father me? Jimmy did that already. He found me on the streets when I just barely a teen and he taught me how to take care of myself. How to live below the radar. And I don't need another father figure."

"He was good to you?" Lukian asked.

She nodded but didn't want to discuss Jimmy anymore.

Lukian embraced her again but didn't hold her too long. "If Eadan hurts you at all, says one cross word to you, looks at you funny, I'll rip his fucking head off. Got it?"

She nearly laughed through her pending tears. "Got it."

Roi offered a lopsided smile. "We have a little sister."

"We do," Lukian said. "Who will be an aunt very soon when our young ones come."

"Possibly a mother herself now that she's found her mate," offered Green.

Roi's expression hardened. "If Eadan even thinks of touching her sexually, I'll tear his dick off and—"

"Enough," Inara snapped. Much to her surprise, both the alpha males shut up. They looked like scolded children as she put one hand on her hip. "No one is hurting Eadan. Got it?"

They nodded and then Roi bit his inner cheek. "From this moment on, right? I mean, we can't get in trouble for what happened fifteen minutes ago, can we?"

Wilson entered and she half expected him to start in on her too. He tipped his head, staring at Lukian and Roi. "Anyone wanna tell me why the colonel and Jon are untying Eadan?"

"You tied him up?" Inara demanded.

Both men in question looked at the ceiling.

Eadan came running in. He pushed power at Lukian and Roi. They toppled over. Gasping, Inara ran to their sides and bent, helping them both up. "Eadan, how could you?"

Eadan looked flabbergasted. "How could I? They tied me up!"

She gave him a stern look. "And you stoop to their level?"

Green laughed. "Eadan, you aren't going to win this argument with her. Your soon-to-be-bride here is genetically related to Lukian and Roi. In simple terms, you have them acting like fathers or brothers to her. Either way, they're overprotective."

Eadan wiped a hand over his face. "I know. I just hoped the paperwork was wrong."

"Wait, you went after her knowing she was related to us, but didn't tell us?" Roi demanded.

"Hey, I was ordered not to tell you," Eadan shot back.

"By who?" Roi narrowed his gaze.

Eadan flashed a wide, mocking smile. "Your father-in-law. Take it up with him."

Inara approached him and stood before him, listening as he ranted about Roi. She waited until he went to take a breath and then stood on her tiptoes, kissing him silent. He returned the kiss tenfold, wrapping his arms around her.

"Mmm," he mouthed against her ear. "Green, can I take her home now?"

"You can."

Eadan placed his hand over hers and led her in the other direction. The rest of the men dispersed. As Inara and Eadan were about to exit the hall she turned, the compulsion to look back too great to resist.

Colonel Brooks was there, his back to her, standing at the far end of the hall. He put his arms out and then in the blink of an eye was gone, vanishing into thin air. She gasped.

Eadan paused. "Inara? You okay, beautiful?"

She debated saying anything. Maybe it was normal for people to disappear around here. After all, they were all sort of odd. "I'm good."

TEN

INARA COULDN'T BELIEVE the size of
Eadan's home. He'd given her the tour and she
was sure she'd get lost if left to fend for herself.
She had half a mind to take his Eighties record
collection and lay them out to make a trail for
herself. She didn't think he'd appreciate that
much. He seemed fond of it.

His bathroom was bigger than most of the
hotel rooms she'd stayed in. The long, hot bath
she'd taken felt glorious. Eadan had so many
shampoos and conditioners to choose from she
half expected a hairdresser to pop out of the
walk-in closet off the bath and offer to do her
hair for her.

She looked at the t-shirt and men's boxers
he'd left on the counter for her. They'd be big

on her but they'd work for now. She held the towel around her, staring at her reflection. She no longer had dark circles under her eyes and already she looked as if she'd put on some much-needed weight.

The healing energy.

Just thinking of how they'd conjured the energy turned her on. Her nipples hardened and moisture pooled at the apex of her thighs. Her body tingled with desire. The buzzing of the bees started again—low but there. And she understood it was partly her doing —her magik.

Seemed silly thinking of herself that way, but it was true. She knew that. She grasped how crazy it was to feel as much as she did for Eadan, considering she'd known him less than a week. None of that mattered to her.

She realized now who he was to her, why she'd been drawing him all her life. She was his woman and he was her man. He was who she'd been waiting for, saving herself for. And she was tired of saving herself.

She wanted the man on the other side of the door, the one doing what he thought was honorable—giving her space and time to adjust.

And it was high time she took what she wanted.

She looked to the clothes he'd left for her, the wheels in her head spinning. Inara exited the bathroom wearing nothing but her towel. Eadan was there, standing in the entranceway to his bedroom, his blue-gray gaze locked on her. "I-Inara?"

How can she be even more beautiful? She heard his voice in her head.

She took a step in his direction. The power intensified as she began to close the distance between them. It ran over her body, centering between her legs, making her breath catch. She inhaled deep, the shifter in her smelling Eadan's arousal.

Damn, he looked even better than he had. He was cleaned up now, wearing nothing but a pair of thin pajama bottoms. His hair was free from the tie he'd worn it in. It was so long. She couldn't wait to see it spilling over her body as he moved above her.

She was obsessed with his torso. The man could do laundry on it, she was sure of it. She wanted to lick him from head to toe.

"I left something for you to wear in there,"

he said, sounding as if he were in pain. "I'll take you and buy you everything you need in the morning."

"All I need is you," she returned, continuing her path to him.

He backed up and hit the doorframe. He closed his eyes.

Control yourself. She needs sleep and food and time to adjust.

"I just need you, Eadan."

He kept his eyes shut.

Think about anything other than her naked. She deserves to be romanced.

"I deserve you."

She's a virgin. Take it slow. And do not tell her you love her. It will scare her away.

Inara couldn't help but warm to him even more. "Eadan."

He opened one eye. "Yes?"

"I love you too."

He gulped and pressed himself against the doorframe more.

Wimp, she pushed with her mind.

He stilled and cracked one eye open to look at her.

She laughed. "Are you going to run from me?"

"I'm considering it," he replied.

"Eadan, I want you and I think you want me too." Pride welled. She'd found her way to the strong female she knew resided in her. She'd just needed the proper motivation. Sex with Eadan did the trick.

He tipped his head back and thumped it against the doorframe. "More than you'll ever know."

"Then what is stopping us?"

He met her gaze and put out his arms as if to shout "back." "Inara, we need to talk. You need to understand what you'd be getting yourself into. This goes beyond any talks about having sex for the first time."

She watched him, feeling very wanton. Energy skimmed over her arms on its way to him. "So tell me what I need to know."

"If we have sex and complete the act, you'll be my wife. No take-backs," he spit out quickly, as if the words had been weighing heavily on him.

His words felt right, as if she'd been waiting for him to say them all along. "Okay."

"Okay?" he asked, shaking his head. "Did you hear me?"

"Loud and clear."

"There is more," he said. "I was married before. You should know that."

"Do you still love her?" she asked. Deep down, she knew the answer but needed to hear him verbalize it.

"Not that way, no. But she's a friend. She'll always only be a friend. She's mated to Roi."

Inara liked that about him. Liked that he'd be mature about his ex. "Ah, so that is part of the reason why Roi is the way he is with you, then?"

Eadan clucked his tongue. "That, and I'm mate to the woman he sees as his little sister."

She laughed and touched his silky hair. The *invisa-bees* pounded at her, pushing over her skin, making her body hum with sexual desire. "Poor thing. Can't catch a break, can you?"

He stepped to her, his hands going to her shoulders, holding her in place. The energy beat at her and she was sure it was doing the same to him. He just seemed better at self-control. "Missy wasn't my true mate. You are."

Magik pulsed between them, its pressure welcomed.

The news she was his true mate only made her want him more. She loosened the towel, letting it fall to the floor. Eadan closed his eyes. "Inara."

"Make me yours, Eadan."

He was on her in an instant. He lifted her, his mouth finding hers. As his tongue eased into her mouth, her legs naturally went around his waist. The ridged, hard outline of his cock pushed against her wet mound.

She didn't need anyone walking her through what to do. It felt right with him. Additional power mixed with the existing, taking the experience to a whole new level. Eadan had added his to it all. Smiling against his lips, she moved, pushing her body to his, wanting more.

His hands kneaded her hips before slinking up her body, coming to a stop just under her breasts. She panted into his mouth as he cupped her breasts, his forefingers and thumbs tweaking her nipples.

EADAN MOVED across the span of the bedroom, holding his mate in his arms. Their joined power, feeding the frenzy he felt in her. Already it seemed as if her hot mouth was wrapped around his cock. It was her magik, enticing him, tempting him and demanding he give her what she wanted.

What he wanted too.

Her long legs wrapped around his waist. Their lips were locked as he hoped their bodies soon would be. She was so wild and wanting that he couldn't resist. He didn't want to resist.

He was almost to the bed when Inara thrust her hands down the front of his pajama bottoms, taking hold of his cock. She drew back from his lips, her eyes wide. "Eadan, it's too big."

He kissed her, silencing her protests. They'd work together. They were made for one another. He laid her down on the bed gently and spread her legs wide. Dark hair covered her mound and he grinned like the cat who had the mouse as he lowered himself, his head even with her pussy. Inhaling, he closed his eyes, breathing in the scent of her cunt. Damn, she smelled good.

She tensed as he stroked along her inner

thigh. Eadan looked up the length of her torso. Their gazes met and she nodded.

Grinning, he licked up her slit, making her squirm on the bed. She moaned as he flicked his tongue over her clit. So responsive. So perfect. So his. He eased a finger into her hot, tight entrance. He pushed through her virgin barrier and she tightened more on his finger. He allowed her time to adjust to having something in her. In the meantime, he sucked gently on her swollen bud, drawing moans from her.

Sexual energy continued to pulsate around them. No surprise. It would also do so when they joined. He couldn't stop the swell of emotions racing through him.

Woman, I love you.

He thrust another finger into her and she cried out, "I love you too!"

As her pussy convulsed around his fingers, Eadan slid up and over her, placing his cock against her core. He kissed her, knowing she could taste herself on his lips. The idea turned him on. As she wrapped her legs around his waist once more, Eadan pushed slowly into her. It seemed to take forever for her body to accept him. He wanted to pound into her but he held back.

He'd never hurt her.

Inara clung to him and then went eerily still. "Eadan."

"Yes, beautiful," he said, straining to keep from coming because of how good she felt wrapped around his cock.

"Am I your wife now?"

He kissed under each of her eyes. "You will be. Once I fill you will my seed. We've already exchanged magik and power. We just need to exchange body fluids now."

She cupped his face. "Then hurry it up."

He did as his mate commanded. He pushed into her and began to move with a slow pace, being gentle with her. Each push, each thrust heightened the magik between them. While they were already linked magikally, they were now in the process of completing the claiming. The threads he'd felt weave between them in the container now felt as if they were unbreakable. They were forged of magik.

He arched his back, his jaw going slack, the energy between them near the bursting point.

Inara cried out, repeating his name as she sank her nails into his skin deeper and deeper.

Eadan grunted, his hips slamming into hers, his cock thrusting in and out of her. She was so tight. He knew he'd have a hard time controlling himself. The power racing back and forth between them did little to help him maintain himself. Reaching down, he stopped and rubbed her clit. Inara tossed her head back, her breasts pushing up at him.

Eadan's power broke free from him, crashing into his mate. She responded, her eyes swirling with various colors, the walls of her pussy fluttering around his cock as she came. He pumped in and out of her and made no move to stop himself as he jetted seed deep in her womb, finishing their bonding ritual.

It was complete.

She was his wife now.

And there were no take-backs.

The room seemed to be on fire with power. It buzzed around him, making his ears ring. His cock hardened again and he looked down at his woman, his lips finding hers as he began to pump into her once more.

He kissed her neck while he continued to

make love to her. Each push left her panting, her eyes wide, a sexy smile easing over her lips.

"Yes," she whispered, kissing his neck in return.

He intended to do as he'd promised. He was going to love her for hours and hours.

ELEVEN

"ARE YOU FULL?" Eadan asked, moving the tray of food from the side of the bed. He'd insisted she eat and eat and eat after they'd showered. She'd burst if he tried to put any more food in her. She caught his hand on his way back from the setting the tray on the table in his room. "Come back to bed."

He looked at her hungrily. "I want to, but you have to be sore."

"Actually, I feel better than ever."

He moved over her and she laid back. His hair, wet from their shared shower, tickled her bare body. At the rate they were going, they'd never leave the bedroom. She was fine with that.

Eadan threaded his hands through the sides of her hair, holding her head in place as he kissed her. He tasted like grapes. She ate at his mouth as the head of his cock nudged at her entrance. She was wet for him. He pushed into her and she arched her back, taking him fully.

The man was dynamite in bed. She didn't think any other could compare and she didn't ever want to try another out. Eadan was hers and she didn't need another man.

Just her mate.

My mate, she mused.

"Mmmhmm," he whispered against her ear, finding a rhythm as he made slow, sweet love to her.

She dug at his back, clinging to him, wanting him to push through her. He increased his pace and within seconds she was on the verge of coming. He pushed in and held deep, his magik caressing hers. Suddenly, it felt as if fingers were rubbing her clit.

Gasping, she came hard, digging her nails into his flesh. She could smell his blood welling. Something primal in her took over. She brought her hand around and licked the blood clean. Her eyes burned for a fraction of a second and the magik around them increased.

Inara looked up at Eadan as he lost control

and exploded in her. He looked surprised. She barely managed to cover her mouth before a sneeze broke free from her. There was a loud boom and the room shook.

Eadan stayed in her and began to laugh.

Inara blinked at him. "W-what happened?"

He glanced to the side. The tray of food that had been on the table was thrown to the other side of the bedroom. That wasn't all. The dresser was on its side. And the table was pressed against the door.

She gasped. "Ohmygod, what happened?"

"You happened." He kissed the tip of her nose. "Your lycan side just claimed me too."

She rubbed her nose. "Why did I sneeze again?"

"I have that effect on you." Eadan kissed the top of her head. "It's our one day anniversary of being man and wife."

"It's probably time you tell me you love me, don't just think it," she said, already knowing he did.

He waggled his brows. "I love you."

She smiled up at him. "I love you too. Mostly for your body. The rest of you is all right too. Though, they should really market an allergy tab for you faeries. I bet pixies wouldn't make me sneeze so much."

Eadan lost it, kissing her neck, making her cackle in his arms as he tickled her. He stopped his sensual assault and looked down at her, his hair spilling all around them. "Inara, when I was getting food from the kitchen, I got a call."

She waited for what he had to say. It looked important.

"About Jimmy."

She closed her eyes. "I know. He's dead."

"That's just it," Eadan said. "PSI doesn't think he is."

She stared up at her husband. "You'll look for him?"

He let out a slow breath. "For you, yes."

"And that is just another reason I love you."

THE END

NY Times & USA TODAY bestselling author *Mandy M. Roth* grew up fascinated by creatures that go bump in the night. From the very beginning, she showed signs of creativity—writing, painting, telling scary stories that left her little brother afraid to come out from under his bed. Combining her creativity with her passion for the paranormal has left her banging on the keyboard into the wee hours of the night.

She's a self-proclaimed Goonie, loves 80s music and movies and wishes leg warmers would come back into fashion. She also thinks the movie *The Breakfast Club* should be mandatory viewing for...okay, everyone. When she's not dancing around her office to the sounds of the 80s or writing books, she can be found designing book covers for NY publishers, small presses, and indie authors.

Mandy writes for The Raven Books, Samhain Publishing, Ellora's Cave Publishing, Harlequin Spice, Pocket Books and Random House/Virgin/Black Lace. Mandy also writes under the pen names Reagan Hawk, Mandy Balde, Rory Michaels and Kennedy Kovit.

To learn more about Mandy, please visit http://www.mandyroth.com or send an email to mandy@mandyroth.com.

For latest news about Mandy's newest releases subscribe to her newsletter

http://www.mandyroth.com/newsletter.htm

Act of Mercy (PSI-Ops Series / Immortal Ops) by Mandy M. Roth

Paranormal Security and Intelligence Operative Duke Marlow has a new mission: find, interrogate and eliminate the target—Mercy Deluca. She's more than he bargained for and Intel has it all wrong. She's not the enemy. Far from it. Intel forgot to mention one vital piece of information—she's Duke's mate. And this immortal alpha werewolf doesn't take kindly to her being in danger.

Excerpt from Act of Mercy (PSI-Ops /
Immortal Ops) by Mandy M. Roth

Duke Marlow finished typing the last of the
reports due in to his handler. Corbin handled
more than one Paranormal Security and Intelligence Operative (PSI-Op) and Duke already
knew he was Corbin's most trying. He enjoyed
getting under the man's skin. Corbin was a
panther shifter and everyone knew cats and
dogs didn't mix well together. As a full-
blooded, born werewolf, Duke tended to get a
kick out of giving Corbin as hard a time as
possible.

Duke rotated his neck, working out a kink as
he sniffed the air, the wolf in him catching the
scent of pending rain. He grinned, knowing
he'd be running free in it soon enough. Well, as
soon as he finished this damn paperwork. He
didn't understand the point of it. It wasn't like
the organization existed to anyone who asked
about it. They were ghosts. Operatives who
never were and never would be, at least
on paper.

What the fuck did they want with a paper trail, then?

The truth of the matter was most of the people within the organization had been there a hell of a long time. Immortality afforded them that luxury. They had some young ones—people under the age of fifty often seemed like pups in his eyes. When you got to his age, most everyone seemed young.

He looked across the main office in PSI headquarters. Rows of desks filled the large bullpen. There was a raised walkway that circled the rounded room. Various doors dotted it. Some were offices. Others interrogation rooms. Some were termed briefing rooms. One was a hallway to restrooms and a kitchen area and the one he disliked visiting most was just past that—the infirmary.

He'd been alive a long time and lost too many people to count that he considered friends, even loved ones. He didn't do well around hospitals or anything of the like. They made him itch. Not as much as planes or anything that flew did.

He fucking hated to fly.

He'd had to fly more times than he'd cared

to for the week prior when he'd been called in to help a fellow PSI-Op. Eadan Daly was someone he'd consider a friend. Eadan was young yet, barely thirty, but like Duke he'd stopped aging. Somehow, Eadan, even at his young age within the immortal world, had managed to find love and happiness. He and his mate were together. That was what was important. Not the how or whys of how they'd come to be that way.

Longing still lingered deep within Duke. He wanted what Eadan had. What so many of the I-Ops had—a mate. Wouldn't happen. Not at his age. If his woman had been out there, he'd have found her by now.

He focused on his reports. While they may be done, they still needed to be emailed. Damn, he hated computers. Everyone around him seemed to love them, but he liked putting pen to paper, not fingertips to keyboard. He took a lot of grief at the office about his aversion to certain technologies. He wasn't a luddite, but the others in PSI seemed to enjoy calling him one.

While he would forever look to be in his mid-thirties, he was considerably older. With that age came the reluctance to accept change with ease. Plus, he was stubborn by nature. And, truth of the matter was, most of what he was given technology-wise ended up breaking. In his opinion it was shit.

He'd seen a lot in his life-span. Some good. Some not so good. And some downright horrifying.

An auburn-haired giant poked his head into the room. Striker McCracken was there, grinning him a grin that said he was ready to be up to no good. He was Dougal only to his momma, who had been buried over a century. Duke knew his real name because he'd actually met the man's mother, way back when. She been a sweet woman who managed to be half her son's size, yet still keep him in line nicely.

"You almost done?" asked Striker, traces of the Scottish accent — which had once been so thick Duke had a difficult time understanding the man — showing through. "I'm positive the bar at the corner has beers with our names on 'em."

With a groan, Duke emailed off his reports. "I fucking hate this thing," he said, as he tried to get the computer to go to sleep, but it kept instantly waking back up.

"Name one thing you *do* like."

"Women," returned Duke.

Laughing, Striker came to his recuse. He took the wireless mouse from Duke's grasp. "It's nae gonna shut down with you bumping the mouse. Here. Let me."

Duke slid back in the chair and then stood. "Keep the fucker."

Striker continued to laugh. "You know, if you tried a little harder, you might actually learn to like the thing."

Sliding his long-time friend a hard look, Duke stood silent. No words needed to be spoken. He'd never bond with his damn computer.

Administrative Control (Immortal Ops) by Mandy M. Roth

As Director of Operations for the Immortal Ops Organization, Colonel Asher Brooks has his hands full. When he's not trying to keep six alpha males in line, he's trying to help them defeat the enemy. Brooks isn't the type to share about his personal life. When given the opportunity to have quality time with the one woman who rocks his world, he takes it, regardless of the cost.

Excerpt from Administrative Control (Immortal Ops)

Colonel Asher Brooks stepped out of the shadows near the old warehouse. The warehouse had been the scene of one hell of a throw-down. Brooks had seen worse.

Much worse.

Truth was, this was hardly a drop in the bucket for him.

The entire area smelled like a mix of death and fish. Neither were great on their own, but combined they were nauseating. He avoided deep breaths as he surveyed the situation.

Carnage.

No one had seen him arrive. They never did. That was how it should be. He needed to be someone the supernaturals he worked with trusted fully without fearing or questioning his loyalty.

His allegiances were his own and not up for debate with the group or the organization. When he'd been brought into the Immortal Ops program, it had not been lightly. The people who thought they had control of it were wrong.

Dead wrong.

Bad decisions had been made. Good people had lost their lives. Brooks was their answer to that. A one-man clean-up crew, if you will.

He checked his watch. The current crew should have already been done with the warehouse and the pier. The I-Ops and the PSI-Ops had left one hell of a mess. He couldn't blame them. Helmuth had an army at the ready and had used a portion of it to attack the I-Ops. Sure, the dead were paranormal thugs hell bent on being part of the new wave of supernaturals, but still, a mess was a mess.

Your men all returned alive. You can't ask for anything better.

He could ask that the violence stop, period, but that would never happen. Since the dawn of time, good had been pitted against evil. It would continue to be until the end. There was no changing it.

He knew. He'd tried.

He walked up behind the cleanup crew, who had yet to notice his arrival. He'd have a talk with them later about that. They should always be on the ready.

"Speed it up," he barked. The two nearest him almost jumped out of their skin.

They needed to get their shit together and clear out soon. He wouldn't risk any of them learning personal information about him. He'd been alive too long and seen too many turncoats to trust anyone with what he held precious.

Or rather, who.

For more information about these titles and other bestselling Mandy M. Roth titles please visit www.MandyRoth.com

Made in the USA
Coppell, TX
06 January 2020

14159749R00116